NORTH

COUNTRY

DETECTIVE

————◆————

TOM BRENNAN

Epicenter Press Inc.
Alaska Book Adventures™

Kenmore, WA

Epicenter Press Inc.
Alaska Book Adventures™

6524 NE 181st St., Suite 2, Kenmore, WA 98028

Epicenter Press is a regional press publishing nonfiction books about the arts, history, environment, and diverse cultures and lifestyles of Alaska and the Pacific Northwest. For more information, visit www.EpicenterPress.com

North Country Detective
Copyright © 2022 by Tom Brennan

Cover design: Scott Book
Interior design: Melissa Vail Coffman

ISBN: 978-1-684920-28-0 (Trade Paperback)
ISBN: 978-1-684920-29-7 (Ebook)

Produced in the United States of America

This book is dedicated to the men and women of Alaska's police forces, the local, state and federal officers who put their lives on the line to keep us safe.

Acknowledgments

———•———

THIS BOOK IS A WORK OF FICTION but the stories on which it is based are true. They are tales that have been told by the news media, public officials and this author, who recounted them in previous books. Many of the tales were genuine tragedies, events that often were accompanied by heroic acts by individuals, police officers and public officials who intervened to prevent worse outcomes. Credit also needs to be given to the editors and news media managers whose courage, determination and talents played critical roles in what became important parts of Alaska's history. Special thanks are due to people whose support and assistance made this book possible. That includes my editors at Epicenter Press, Lael Morgan and Phil Garrett, retired Colonel of the Alaska State Troopers Tom Anderson, whose vast experience in law enforcement helped me identify fascinating cases and knowledgeable people, and my wife Marnie, whose encouragement, love of adventure and challenge first brought me to Alaska and made it possible for me to stay here through the years.

Chapter 1

GEORGE TALLENT, AN ALASKA NATIVE BOY new to Anchorage approached the junior high school door timidly, hands buried deep in the pockets of faded bluejeans. He looked up at the arching entrance and muttered: "I hope I'm ready for this."

Behind him came Rick Albert, a white boy his age, similarly dressed and equally as nervous. Though they wouldn't know it for some time, they were *exactly* the same age, both born on July 5, 1942. It was then September 6, 1956 and they were both 14 years old with light blond hair.

"That's what I was thinking," Rick said, nodding. "I hope *I'm* ready."

George laughed and looked intensely at his new friend. "What are you worried about? You're white and were probably born here. I'm an Eskimo from Kiana, a village way up North on the Kobuk River. You should fit right in with these kids—and the teachers too. Me? Maybe, and maybe not."

Rick shook his head. "I'm not so sure of that. I was born in Massachusetts, but my family moved to Minnesota when I was in grade school. Dad is in the military. Brought us to Alaska two years ago. He's an Army mechanic and came here to work on the airplanes flying back and forth to Russia. My mom wanted us to be in Anchorage so we could be near him. Anchorage is a long way from Minnesota—and that Alaska Highway is the bumpiest road I ever saw. No pavement anywhere."

"You like it here?" George asked, referring to Anchorage but gesturing toward the school door and the broad and brightly-lit hallway beyond. His new friend nodded and walked beside him as George moved toward the entrance and pulled the door open.

"Yeah, I really do. Mom loves the place, especially all the wild-life and the great scenery. We had a black bear in our yard this morning. He was trying to get into the trash cans when they were full and waiting for pickup. Dad had to chase him away so I could get out of the house to catch the school bus."

"We love it too," George said. "Those mountains behind the city are great. The view is a lot like the one from Kiana but things are a little closer together here. Will your family be staying in Anchorage?"

"I don't know," Rick replied. "Sure hope so. My dad took me fishing when the salmon came in this summer. Caught some nice kings. It was a hoot and I'd like to do more of that. How about you? How come you're in Anchorage? You been here long?"

"About two months. My parents moved us here so I could go to high school in the city and dad could get a job at the Army base. With the big war over and the Russians making like they want another one, the economy is booming and dad wanted to get in on it. Not many jobs in Kiana these days. And Mom wasn't too happy about the village school. Not enough kids and only one teacher. There really isn't any high school, just a few older kids that meet with the teacher when he's off work. People get by on catching fish, hunting and trapping game, but there's no way to make money. We need a lot of things from the Sears catalog and you have to pay for those."

"Welcome to the city," Rick said, shaking George's hand and gesturing down the wide hallway. "Hope you make a fortune."

The Eskimo boy laughed and strode beside him. "I'm not plan-ning on that. Love to have it happen but I'll take what comes. Let's see what the inside of this place looks like."

Rick smiled broadly. "Well, here we are at Anchorage High School. Assuming you are a freshman like me, we are part of the class of 1960. Let's go in."

"I am and let's go."

Chapter 2

———•———

A MIDDLE-AGED FEMALE TEACHER MET THE BOYS in the hallway and motioned them to move away from the door. "You kids need to get in here," she said, her arm waving urgently. "There's a moose in the schoolyard and some dogs are barking at it, getting the thing worked up. We don't want him to start charging people. Somebody could get hurt."

The two boys raced further into the building and down a secondary hallway to a window overlooking the schoolyard. Moose were nothing new to them; the huge animals often wandered into the city and spent days and nights munching on the leaves and twigs of young birch trees in people's yards. They could see the moose, a young female, standing outside the school and eyeing a pair of nervous and rapidly pacing dogs behind a chain-link fence near the back of the yard. Just before the start of classes the boys headed for their homeroom.

An attractive woman with a welcoming smile approached the boys. "Can I help you find something?" she asked.

George started to answer but Rick held up a hand to cut him off. "Yes," Rick said. "We are just starting here in first grade and looking for our classroom.

"Then follow me. I'm Miss Stanford and I'll be your teacher. Our classroom is at the end of the hall on the right hand side."

"We'll be right behind you," Rick replied.

As the teacher turned away the boys noticed she had a very attractive backside. Rick pointed to her butt and held his hands over his heart as they walked. Then a large hairy hand descended on his shoulder and pulled him aside.

Miss Stanford turned to the man, who was obviously a teacher irate at Rick's behavior. "Is there a problem?" she asked.

"Just a little horseplay. They were having some fun. I think it's over with. You might want to take them to your classroom now."

"Come along," she said to the boys. "And knock off the foolishness. You can have fun later."

"Yes ma'am," George said, thoroughly chastened.

The two boys followed Miss Stanford into her classroom and took adjacent seats at the closely-spaced desks. She stood, walked to the blackboard and wrote her name in chalk as the boys tried to avoid staring at her shapely butt. Their education had begun.

Chapter 3

A FTER NEARLY FOUR HOURS OF CLASSES A BELL RANG to signal the lunch break. George followed Rick into the dining room and—at his invitation—followed him into the food line, then trailed behind as Rick made his way to seats at a rapidly-filling table.

"Tell me about yourself," Rick said as they sat down and spread their paper-wrapped lunches around the table surface. "What's it like in Kiana? Lots of wild animals?"

George looked around at their table-mates. Like many Alaska Natives new to the city, he was painfully aware he was different from most of his classmates and replied softly: "It's cold country, at least in winter. Not many people around, just a few villages here and there. Nearest city is Fairbanks about 400 miles south. Lots of caribou and moose, salmon in the river that runs past the village. Pretty nice, actually. I spent all the time I could outdoors; hunting, fishing, hiking in the summer, skiing and snowshoeing in winter. How about you? What's it like where you come from."

Rick was surprised by the question. Most people wanted to know little more than where one lived in the city and how long you had been in Alaska. For them life starts when you reach Alaska. Everything else is just preparation.

"I was born in Ayer, Massachusetts, way on the other side of the country, a little town outside an Army base, Fort Devens, where my dad worked. Lots of kids, good place to grow up. I used to play a lot of basketball in winter and baseball in spring and summer. Made money setting pins in a bowling alley. Nice beaches on Cape Cod, where the ocean starts. My folks used to rent a cottage there every summer. My mother and I stayed there in the warmer months and dad drove back and forth to the Army base while we were at the beach."

"Then we moved to Eleveth," Rick said, "a small town in Minnesota, a lot like northern Alaska in a way. Gets fifty below zero sometimes in winter. Never that cold in Anchorage that I know of."

Anchorage is a city in Southcentral Alaska where the winter temperature rarely gets below zero. In summer the mercury often reaches sixty degrees or more, sometimes seventy. After the extremes of Interior Alaska, where the temperature frequently reached fifty below in mid-winter, George Tallent and his family were pleasantly surprised by the moderate year-round weather.

George nodded at Rick's comments about Minnesota and Northern Alaska. He knew where Massachusetts was, had read about it in his preparation for formal schooling, but wasn't sure what part of the world Minnesota was in. Alaska is a huge state and, like many Alaska youngsters, his knowledge of geography was primarily about where the Alaska communities lay. In the Alaskan mind the world was divided into two large regions. One was the vast area of Alaska, a territory covering 663,000 square miles. The other was what Alaskans call "Outside," meaning everything outside of Alaska—the entire rest of the world.

George was accustomed to deep cold in Alaska's Interior but Anchorage temperatures were moderated by the nearby ocean and rarely saw anything worse than twenty below zero. "We got fifty below in Kiana sometimes," he said.

Rick shook his head. "Think I'll stick with Anchorage. Banana belt, my dad calls it, and that's fine with me."

"I almost didn't come to Anchorage High," George added. "My folks wanted me to go to a church school but I didn't want any part of that. Those teachers have a bug up their butt about religion. I think I could handle services on Sunday but not preaching every day. Dad and Mom finally gave in and said I could come here if I keep my grades up. Knock on wood but I think I can do it."

"Is there a church in Kiana?"

"No, but the missionaries come through a lot. On a regular basis, actually. Too regular if you ask me."

"You didn't like them?"

"Oh they're OK," George answered. "They're good people, I know. But when they're around kids they get kind of preachy."

"Don't they have kids of their own?" Rick asked.

"Oh yeah, they talk about them a lot but don't bring them when they're traveling around. I wish they did. I'd love to hear what their kids say about them."

"You think that might be bad?"

"Oh probably not, but you never know."

When another bell rang, the two youngsters dropped their food trays into a plastic tub and headed back to class.

Chapter 4

————+————

R ICK AND GEORGE BECAME FAST FRIENDS and grew closer together with many shared experiences as time went by. A week before the start of their sophomore year, Rick showed up at George's house early one morning and threw a piece of wadded paper at his friend's bedroom window. The wad, weighted with a clod of dirt, landed with a thud.

George peered out, raised the window and asked in a whisper: "What's up?"

Rick waved at him to come outside. He mouthed the words "I have an idea."

George's dad had already left for work and his mother was working on a breakfast to be served to her three children when they later came down from their bedrooms. When George entered the kitchen she gave him a surprised look which George responded to by holding his finger to his lips. "I'll be right back," he said. "I have to talk to my friend Rick for a few minutes."

George opened the dining room door and stepped outside. He gave Rick a quizzical look.

"We need to try out for the basketball team," he said.

George frowned. "Rick, you know I'm no good at sports."

"That's because you never play them. You're strong. You move fast and you're well-coordinated. Let's shoot a few hoops and do a little workout. You might surprise yourself."

Rick reached behind the shrubbery in the Tallent family yard and pulled out a basketball. "I brought this along just in case," he said. "Let's get started."

George laughed. "Oh, what the hell. OK. But first I have to eat."

THE TWO BOYS WALKED THE FOUR blocks to the schoolyard with Rick dribbling the basketball most of the way, occasionally throwing it to George who quickly threw it back each time.

The following week Rick and George went to the high school for tryouts. They were met by the coach and nine other youngsters who were trying out for the team. The coach directed the players through a series of exercises then waved them to take seats on a bench.

"Mr. Tallent," he said, "can I talk to you a minute in private?"

George was pretty sure he knew what was coming and followed the coach in visible state of dejection.

"Son," the coach said. "I really appreciate your effort to become a player on the team. And I can tell that you've been trying hard. But playing basketball is not what you are best at. You are not bad but I don't have enough openings on the team for players at your skill level. If you don't mind joining us but not playing I can offer you another option, if you are interested."

"We'll need a team manager," the coach said, "somebody to keep track of the equipment, chase balls if they go out of bounds and get everything back into lockers after training and games. You would get to wear a uniform and attend all workouts and games."

George clapped his hands. "I'll take it," he said. "I know I'm not much of a player but I'd like to stay with the team, especially if I can be on the bus for out-of-town games."

George was not surprised to be rejected as a player. The young Eskimo boy was strong and well-coordinated but did not have much athletic ability, had never seen the need to develop it while living in the village where physical fitness was essential to survival but playing games was not. The title of manager was essentially honorific but the job would allow George to wear a uniform, travel Southcentral Alaska with the team and participate in its social activities.

He was secretly humiliated by the assignment, but George enjoyed the duties and did his job faithfully. He began working out in private to improve his visible musculature and prepare himself for a physically challenging job in the future.

"You OK with that, being manager instead of a player?" Rick asked, his tone implying that George might be angry about what seemed a menial job.

"It's alright," George answered. "I'd rather *play* basketball but I'll settle for just staying with the team."

George made up for his meager basketball skills with a sharp mind and innate talent for solving math and science problems. His teachers were impressed with his abilities and encouraged him to make the most of them. They moved him into advanced classes whenever any were available. Some made a point of spending extra time with him during what were called study periods, hours when most students were getting a head start on their day's homework.

George and Rick remained close friends throughout their high school years. In their free time they went fishing in summer, cross-country skiing in winter and hiking in all the between times. Both considered the Alaska back-country to be an invitation to adventure, a place where young men could challenge themselves and do so in a place of great beauty with all the attractions of wild country.

Chapter 5

B OB ATWOOD WAS THE PUBLISHER of Alaska's largest newspaper, The Anchorage Times. He was deeply engrossed in composing an editorial for the next day's paper when Diddy Beaulieu, his secretary, opened the office door, stuck her head in and whispered "Governor Gruening is here and would like to talk to you."

"By all means," Atwood said. "Send him in." Gruening was governor of the Alaska Territory and Atwood would make time for him whenever the governor wanted it. He slipped the editorial into a desk drawer and stood to welcome his distinguished guest.

"To what do I owe the pleasure?" Atwood asked.

"We need to talk," Gruening said. "I've had it up to here with those bureaucrats in Washington."

"Now what?" Atwood asked, shaking his head and gesturing to Gruening to take a seat.

"They make all our decisions for us and they don't listen to us. The shippers run everything—and we pay whatever prices on merchandise that they choose to stick us with. The cost of living is through the roof here in a place where people mostly live off the land. It shouldn't be that way."

Atwood grimaced. It was a never-ending problem. Alaska was a long way from what its residents called The Lower 48 and the shipping companies that carried cargo to the territory had no competitors and could therefore dictate whatever prices people had to pay for the food and goods they needed. The state's only railroad had a similar monopoly and people living in Interior Alaska and the widely-separated small communities along its route were economic captives.

"I know just what you mean, Governor. It bugs me too. We've been part of the United States since this country bought it from the Russians in 1867. But after all that time we still have no real airports, no cities, not even a hospital that can handle tuberculosis patients. If somebody catches TB they either have to stay here until they die or try to get on a steamer headed for Seattle."

"Bob," Gruening said. "It's time we got serious about Alaska becoming a state. You've been campaigning for statehood for many years and doing a great job of it. You've been chairman of the Statehood Committee and you've traveled the state whipping up sentiment for statehood. Alaska has tremendous potential. We have gold, copper, coal and fish, maybe even oil. But those things will never be developed for their full potential unless we can run our own show and take the power away from those federal bureaucrats who run things."

"Well, thank you Governor. I appreciate the kind words. Any ideas on where we should go from here?"

Gruening glanced over his shoulder as an indication of secrecy, meaning Atwood should not mention his visit. "Bob, things are looking up. "Doug McKay is out as Secretary of the Interior and he was a major obstacle to Alaska statehood. He was dead set against it for reasons that I don't fully understand. But Fred Seaton from Nebraska took his place and he is a friend of Alaska's. I know you've talked to him about statehood for Alaska more than once."

"I have," Atwood said. "Many times."

"Seaton will back us when we make our play," Gruening said. "And now is the time. I'm sure of it. We need to get serious about becoming a state," the governor added. "Bob Bartlett tells me the more powerful people in Washington are telling him the time is right." Bartlett was Alaska's delegate to Congress, its link to the Washington power structure.

"I know Congress has turned us down seven times already," Gruening said, "but attitudes are changing in much of the country. I think Americans are ready. And the dynamics are ripe. Both houses of Congress are controlled by Democrats, and Hawaii wants statehood just as much as Alaska does. Alaska's people are mostly Democrats but Hawaii leans to the Republican side. If Alaska and Hawaii were a package deal, if they achieved statehood at the same time, the deal might just be acceptable to both parties and doable. Maintaining the political balance would make it possible, and a package deal like that would be acceptable to both sides."

"Hawaii wants statehood as much as we do and it might have to be part of the package, but the two territories are at opposite ends of the Pacific Ocean and would offset each other geographically as well as politically. Hawaii is a conservative territory and Alaska leans the other way. If we both got statehood, that would avoid changing the political balance in Congress and, really, in the nation. I think it's doable right now."

"What do you suggest?" Atwood asked. "How do we go about it? How do we close the deal?"

Gruening rubbed his hands together with a broad smile on his face. "Double down on your articles and editorials, Bob. And develop all support from the people that you can put together. Whip them up and bring pressure on Congress to grant us statehood."

Atwood strode to his office window and looked out thoughtfully over Fourth Avenue, the small commercial center of Anchorage, Alaska's largest community. He turned to Gruening and asked: "Any thoughts on what it would take to get that done?"

"A few," Gruening replied. "Our politically active people are all in small, scattered communities and Native villages. I could work on bringing them onboard if you could rally the business people. They are pretty scattered and their businesses are small. But all of them buy their supplies from companies in the Lower 48. If we could mobilize them we just might be able to bring enough pressure on the suppliers to support us."

"Wow," Atwood said, rubbing his hands together. "It would take a lot of work and some salesmanship but I think the people of Alaska would be on board if you asked them to. If you will do that, take the lead, then I'll back you one hundred percent."

"You bet," Gruening said. "I'll give it everything I've got."

Chapter 6

—•—

THE NEXT DAY THE PEOPLE OF ANCHORAGE and the surrounding area unfolded their newspapers and read a double-decker all-caps headline blaring: GRUENING ARGUES STATEHOOD TIME HAS ARRIVED

The article announced that Governor Ernest Gruening had taken the lead in what looked to be an all-out effort to win statehood for Alaska.

"Now is the time," he told The Anchorage Times in an exclusive interview. "The people of Alaska have waited too long to achieve full citizenship in the United States of America.

"We have been second-class citizens for far too long. We deserve to have full representation in Congress instead of just a delegate. Bob Bartlett has done a fine job representing us in Congress but he has little power other than to be a lonely voice at the back of the hall. No more."

The article went on to list a raft of grievances Alaska had suffered in its lowly condition as a territory owned by the nation. The notion of ownership was itself very painful and could not be further tolerated. It said the northernmost territory had waited too long and its people were ready to take on the serious responsibilities of statehood. They would do whatever was necessary, bear whatever burden, and as Atwood wrote in his fiery editorial: "Now is the time. Let's do it."

The editorial also argued that if granting Hawaii statehood would make Alaska's membership in the union more palatable to the nation, Hawaii should be brought in around the same time, maybe a few months after Alaska.

When the telephone on his desk buzzed, his secretary told him: "Governor Gruening is on the line."

Atwood said "Hello" and Gruening's voice boomed from the receiver: "Thank you!" the governor said, and promptly hung up.

Chapter 7

———◆———

TWO WEEKS LATER GRUENING AND ATWOOD FLEW together in a small plane to the village of Bethel in Southcentral Alaska. Gruening was scheduled to give a speech to a small group of statehood advocates and Atwood was there to cover the event for his newspaper. The Anchorage Times didn't normally cover events in Bethel—its attention primarily focused on the small city of Anchorage—and its reaching out to write about a speech in the distant village was an indicator of something important in the air, a turning point in a years-long effort.

The day after their return to Anchorage, Gruening gave a stemwinder of a speech to the all-male Anchorage Rotary Club, a weekly gathering of community and business leaders. Gruening's words seemed to take the Rotarians by surprise and their enthusiasm was huge. As he finished the crowd came to its feet, something the genteel Rotarians normally only did when they were about to leave. But this time they applauded and cheered wildly. As their sounds began to fade, Gruening pointed to Atwood, seated next to him at the head table, and added:

"Before I take my seat I want to thank my good friend Bob Atwood for the leadership he has taken in the long-awaited drive for statehood. A lot of work remains but thanks in large part to Bob Atwood we are getting off to a great start."

A RENEWED WAVE OF CHEERING AND APPLAUSE ERUPTED and Gruening grabbed Atwood's arm, brought him to his feet and raised their conjoined arms into the air. Gruening and Atwood could both be seen saying "Thank you" but the crowd noise drowned out both their words.

On July 19, 1957 California-based Richfield Oil Company announced that it had discovered a significant amount of crude oil near the Swanson River on the Kenai Peninsula south of Anchorage. The announcement generated unprecedented excitement in the territory since it suggested that oil might soon become the underpinnings for a thriving Alaska economy.

The news of the discovery went nationwide and touched off a rush of oil companies to acquire oil and gas leases in Alaska. As Bob Atwood later wrote, the discovery at Swanson River and its rush for leases would dwarf Alaska's famed Klondike gold rush of the late 1890s.

When Bob Atwood heard news of the discovery he ran to his typewriter and tapped out a breathless editorial. "This may be the Discovery Day everybody has been waiting for," he wrote. "Hang on . . . Alaska is going around a sharp curve and is heading down a new road of development such as has never been seen before."

When Richfield later confirmed that its Alaska discovery was indeed a major one, the entire business and civic community of the territory began an extended celebration. The territory seemed to be assured of jobs and new investments for generations to come. And that promise would indeed prove to be true.

Alaska's first governor after statehood in 1959, William A. Egan, would later say the Swanson River discovery provided "the economic justification for statehood for Alaska" and would fulfill the dreams of those who fought to make Alaska the 49th state of the union over the opposition of those who thought the northern territory would be an economic burden on the rest of the nation.

Chapter 8

———•———

Geoorge Tallent and Rick Albert were sophomores in high school when Richfield discovered oil at Swanson River. They were amazed to hear and read that the discovery would change Alaska forever and start an economic boom likely to last for years. Though it wasn't known at the time, Cook Inlet would ultimately be dotted with large steel platforms supporting drilling rigs and living quarters for the crews that worked on them. The rigs were designed to tap the vast pools of oil deep beneath the silty waters. That success, in turn, won interest from explorers in oil possibilities throughout the vast state, including the flat plain near the Arctic Ocean at Alaska's northern edge and northwest of George Tallent's old village home in Kiana.

One fall day in their junior year George and Rick's teacher rapped on her desk for attention.

"Boys and girls," she said, "we have a very special experience for you today, a visit from one of Alaska's leaders. Please pay attention."

The teacher gestured toward the classroom door where a man's face was peering through the glass. The man opened the door and walked in.

"Hello," he said in greeting to the youngsters.

"Class, this is William Egan, one of our territory's leaders, a man who is working for Alaska to be successful in its quest to become a state of the American Union. And I am sure he will one day be successful. He is here today because he is my personal friend and offered to meet with you."

The classroom erupted in wild applause. All of the children knew Egan's name and the fact that he was one of Alaska's greatest leaders. The loud applause was unusual for a classroom and the teacher waved for them to keep it down. She worried what the other teachers in the school must be thinking.

"Thank you," Egan said. "As Miss Alexander told you I am here today because she and I are friends and you are her students, but I also wanted to be here because I strongly believe that it is vitally important that young Alaskans be aware of the journey that our territory has begun. This is a very important time in our history, one you young folks will remember for the rest of your lives."

"Many of us have been working for a very long time to end Alaska's territorial status and to make it a full member of the United States. When that happens—and I believe it will be soon—Alaska will become the 49th state of the American union."

"When that happens our new state will have two members of the United States Senate and one member of the national House of Representatives."

"As the years go on we will need new leaders," Egan said, "people to fill those jobs, to go to Washington and to present the viewpoints of the people of Alaska to the United States Congress and, indirectly, to the rest of the United States. I hope you young people will support our leaders and help them achieve Alaska's destiny in the community of states and in the world. Keep in mind that we are closer to Russia, China and Japan than we are to many parts of the United States. For that reason we need to think both nationally and globally."

Throughout Egan's impromptu speech young Rick Albert sat nodding in his chair. He understood what the man was saying and silently vowed to take it very much to heart.

Chapter 9

JUST A FEW MONTHS LATER—ON MAY 28, 1958—the United States Senate did in fact pass an enabling bill allowing Alaska to become the 49th member of the United States of America. The news from Washington was received with joy all across the huge territory. Drinking was widespread, even among some of its younger residents. George, Rick and their school friends were able to secure a case of beer which they carried to a drove of trees near their homes and drank until they became sick. When they were able to rouse themselves and head home later that day, they crept into their houses and went quietly to bed, careful not to attract the attention of their parents. But most Alaskan adults were busily engaged in their own joyful celebrations of statehood and paid little attention. Acceptance into the union's family of states was one of the most memorable occasions in the lives of all Alaskans and behavior that might ordinarily have attracted displeasure from parents was forgiven or ignored that day.

When Alaska's long statehood campaign came to a successful conclusion and the territory was officially admitted to the Union, it was awarded three new political positions, one membership in the United States House of Representatives and two seats in the U.S. Senate. The first election of statehood was held in November of 1958 and Alaska's first three members of Congress were chosen. In January young Rick Albert listened on the radio as Ralph Rivers of Fairbanks was sworn in to become the official congressman from Alaska and Bob Bartlett and Ernest Gruening became the first two United States senators. Rick decided that day he would eventually take one of those distinguished jobs in Washington. And since Alaska had only one House seat and two in the Senate—and the Senate jobs paid the most—he assumed the one-of-a-kind seat would be less prestigious but might be the easiest to get.

When Rick's father asked one day what he wanted to do in life, he was quick to answer: "Well, first I'd like to get a job in the oil industry to make some money but eventually I'd like to get into politics! I want to run for office."

His father was taken aback. He considered giving up an oil job for political office a step down. "Why politics, son?"

"Because you can make things happen," the boy replied.

"What kind of things?"

"Almost anything," he said. "You can make things happen for your friends and for your family and everybody else. If you know what you are doing there are no limits."

A puzzled look crossed Rick's father's face. The elder Albert had been a shopkeeper for most of his career and was happy to see new jobs opening in Southcentral Alaska, relatively near the family home in Anchorage. An oil industry job seemed like a good career that would make the boy a nice salary, but why would he want to start a lucrative oil career and quit that for politics, of all things. Keeping in the public eye for years on end seemed to him a dreadful fate, but he shrugged and thought: Somebody has got to do it. If my son wants that kind of life, he can have it. Not for me.

That night after dinner Rick's father stopped by his son's bedroom where the boy was deep into his homework.

"Mind if I interrupt for a minute, son?"

"Come on in, Dad. Anytime."

Rick's father took a seat awkwardly on the side of the boy's bed. "I've been thinking about what you said about going into politics and running for office."

Rick laughed and turned in his swivel chair. "I don't know that I'll ever get a chance to do that," he said. "Not many people actually do. But I would love to give it a try if something comes open when I'm old enough to run."

The elder Albert squeezed his hands together and said: "I just wanted you to know that if the opportunity comes your way and you decide to run for something, I will back you up one hundred per cent. I'll help anyway I can, even with money if you need it."

Rick was delighted but tried to conceal his enthusiasm. "If I do run for something I'll definitely need a little money for the campaign. When the time comes, if it does,I will come to you first. It would mean a lot to me if you were my first donor. If you give me a check I might never cash it."

"Thank you Rick," his father said with a laugh. "I'd be glad to do that. But to make sure you use the money for the campaign, I'll give you cash; no check. Just let me know when the time comes and I'll be there for you."

Rick leaped across the room and hugged his father fiercely. "Thanks Dad," he said.

Chapter 10

———•———

Toward the end of his junior year, George was walking past the Anchorage hardware store when he noticed a 'Help Wanted' sign in the window. On a whim he walked in, applied for the job and was hired. His duties were mostly stocking shelves, carrying hardware from the storeroom to the front of the store and occasionally waiting on customers. The store was sizable and modern, with bright lighting and shelves that spread across the entire room.

After a week he realized the job came with certain advantages, one that he handled money, cash that his co-workers treated casually and with minimal attention to accounting. The other advantage became obvious when an attractive young woman his age came rushing along an aisle where he was stacking merchandise. She had long blond hair, a nice figure and pretty face.

"Hello," he said, admiration in his voice. "Who are you?"

The girl spun, stopped and looked him over, her eyes appraising the handsome, muscular young man. "I'm Cindy," she said. "My dad owns this place. You must be new. I've never seen you here."

His eyes scanned Cindy from head to toe. "Just started last week. I hope you come into the store a lot. You brighten up the place."

Cindy flashed him a broad smile. "I come here quite a bit. Are you in school?"

"I'm a junior at Anchorage High. How about you?"

"I'm a junior at Holy Cross High," she answered, her face pouting. "I wanted to go to Anchorage but my dad insisted I go to a Catholic school. The classes are kind of interesting there but the social life is dreadful."

George laughed. "I get off at four. Can I buy you a soda or something around then?"

"I'd love that. The place down on the corner, Bert's?"

"I'll see you there."

Cindy turned pertly and headed off to see her father in the store office.

George waited alone in a corner booth while Cindy lingered with a girlfriend two blocks away. She didn't want to seem too anxious and felt being a few minutes late would show the handsome Eskimo boy she had a busy schedule. She entered Bert's Drugstore at 4:10, spotted George and walked slowly to his booth, sliding dramatically into the bench opposite him. The store was large by Anchorage standards, had several merchandise aisles, a drug counter and a half-dozen teenagers seated in nearby booths. The three boys in one booth took stealthy glances at Cindy; the girls pointedly ignored her.

"Hello," Cindy said. "Have you ordered yet? I'd like a Pepsi."

"That sounds good," George said. I believe I'll have the same thing." He stood, walked to the counter and ordered the two beverages.

When he returned she asked: "How do you like working at the hardware store?"

He handed her a plastic cup filled with the soft drink, brushing her hand as he did. The touch brought a knowing smile to Cindy's face. "The work is good and the people are nice," George said, "but the pay isn't much to brag about."

"I know," she said. "I think some of the people make up for it a little bit by tapping the register."

"Hmm," he said. "I wondered about that."

"Are you thinking of doing that?" she asked, a quizzical look on her face.

"No way," he said, "I'm no crook, at least by my standards."

"Hah," she said. "Glad to hear it. But, you know, sometimes things happen and you need money."

"What do you mean by that?" he countered, his voice defensive.

"Nothing," she said. "You never know what's going to happen. Have you decided what you are going to do after high school?"

George started to answer, then hesitated. He had never given much thought to what he might do after graduating. He assumed he would get a job of some kind or perhaps even join the military. He was interested in the idea of going on to college, but that seemed beyond his reach. The cost would be insurmountable.

Chapter 11

ONE DAY RICK APPROACHED GEORGE WITH AN IDEA on how to make some money. "Remember what I told you about Cindy warning me against taking money from the cash register?"

"Yeah," George said. "Did she change her mind?"

"No," George replied, but I've got another idea."

Rick rubbed his hands together and said: "Taking from the register is too much like criminal stuff for me. It would really bother me. But there might be another way that we could make a few bucks without really hurting anybody."

George gave his friend a quizzical look. "Tell me more."

"That store is filled with stuff," Rick replied. "There is way more than the clerks could ever sell. If it just sits there and rots, that wouldn't help anybody. If a little piece just disappeared, one here and one there, nobody would know and nobody would be hurt. But those tools especially are worth money and we could make a few bucks by selling a few to people who need them."

"That sounds interesting," George said. "Show me how it would work and let's see if you can really make money at it without getting caught."

"I'll need your help," Rick answered. He then explained what he had in mind and left the store.

George took a small wrench from a shelf, wrapped it in brown paper and left the packet near a trash can in the alley behind the store. Fifteen minutes later Rick entered the alley, cautiously checked to make sure nobody was watching and picked it up.

The operation seemed a success, so George put a few more tools inside wrapping paper and dropped them behind the store. Rick soon took them away and the following Saturday met with George at the drugstore. After they ordered their sodas Rick handed him a five-dollar bill, as much money as George made in two full days of work.

"There's a lot more where that came from," he said. "Keep those tools coming."

The two boys continued their scheme for another week until George was approached by the store manager and asked what he was up to.

"What do you mean?" George asked.

The manager frowned deeply. "Joe Finnegan says he saw you take a tool, wrap it in paper like it was sold and drop it in the alley. He said a kid came by to pick it up and walk away with it. The kid looked a lot like Rick Albert."

George burst into tears. "I'm sorry, sir. I didn't want to do that but my buddy talked me into it."

The manager frowned, rubbed his chin and said: "You're a good worker and I'd like to keep you on." George could tell from the man's tone that he was suppressing anger. "But I can't do that if you keep stealing things. One more time and you are out on your ear."

George was devastated. Weeping, he pulled out his wallet and handed the manager a five-dollar bill.

"Here," he said. "I'm sorry. I never should have done it. I knew better. I just shouldn't have done it. Never in a million years. I had another five dollars but I spent it."

The manager felt bad for the boy but accepted the bill, folded it and stuffed it into a pocket. "I'm not going to fire you, son" he said. "Just don't ever take anything out of here that doesn't belong to you."

George swore that he would not. To make sure he didn't, the manager called a friend of his, Walter Parker, a sergeant in the Alaska State Troopers, and asked him to talk to the boy and make sure he stayed on the straight and narrow.

Chapter 12

———•———

THE NEXT DAY WAS A SATURDAY AND GEORGE WAS STUDYING in his room when his mother answered the door and was surprised to find a uniformed State Trooper asking to speak to her son. The officer was an older man with grizzled face and a demeanor that told Alicia Tallent he was there on serious business.

"Is he in trouble?" she asked.

"No, not right now, but his employer is worried about him. He asked me to give George a little lecture and make sure he knows right from wrong."

She pointed up the stairs and said: "First door on your left. Give him a good talking to and let me know if there is anything I should do."

The officer tapped lightly on the bedroom door and George opened it, his jaw dropping when he saw the man in his blue and gray uniform. "Hello," he said in a tremulous voice.

"Can I come in?" Sergeant Parker asked. George swung the door wide and pointed to an empty armchair, a worried look on his face. Parker seated himself and looked around; the room was a typical teenager's lair with walls left bare at his mother's insistence.

"I'm told you've been stealing tools from the store where you work, Benson's Hardware."

George's heart fell through his shoes and tears gushed from his eyes. "I did," he said, "but I'll never do it again. I swear."

"I'm glad to hear that, son," Parker said. "You don't want to get started down that road. It can be really hard to come back."

"I . . . I know that sir, and I won't." George sat motionless for ten minutes while the State Trooper talked to him about honesty and the evils of stealing.

"I was a kid like you once and got into a similar jam," Parker said. "I thought about it a lot and decided I wanted to be a good person and live my life on the right side of the law. So after I finished high school I trained to become a police officer and was recruited to join the Alaska State Troopers. You might want to think about something like that for your own future. Your boss told me a lot about you and I think you'd make a damn fine Trooper if you stop trying to get something for nothing. You want to be on the right side of the law. *Enforcing* the law is a very satisfying job, one you can be proud of doing. Not all jobs are like that."

"And," he said, his head nodding and voice dropping to its telling-a-secret level. "we've had Alaska Natives in the Village Public Safety Officer program for years. But we've never had an Eskimo, Indian or Aleut as a Trooper. That time is going to come and you might want to apply when you are old enough."

Parker then stood and shook young George's hand, an event the boy had never imagined and would remain in memory throughout his life. When the officer left, George leaned against the bedroom door with tears sliding down his face.

The next afternoon George met Rick in the schoolyard, told him about the State Trooper's visit and, to change the subject before his friend could ask a question about his time with the officer, George asked Rick how he enjoyed the class president's job.

"It's not bad," Rick replied, a widening smile on his face. "Keeps me busy and there are a few perks."

"Like what?" George knew there were advantages to office but Rick's smile hinted something unusual.

Rick looked around to make sure no adults were listening. "The girls hang around me and some don't mind if I feel their boobs. Sometimes you get a little more than that. You should run for office."

George laughed. "Not for me. I like what I'm doing and would just as soon get my feels the hard way, by wooing the girls. And," though smiling, he pushed a finger hard against Rick's chest, "keep your hands to yourself around Cindy. She and I are going steady these days and I don't want anything to mess it up."

"Don't worry about that," Rick chuckled. "I know what's OK and what's not. Messing with your best friend's girl is not my thing. That is a good way to get pulverized and run out of town. I think you and Cindy might just get married someday and I want to be there when you do."

"I don't know about that," George replied, reddening. "We never talk about getting married, just going steady for a long time. And I'd rather she not know that you're feeling up her friends."

"I don't let anybody know what I'm doing when I'm enjoying myself that way," Rick countered. "It's important. The girls insist on it and they are right. Getting caught messing with one could get a guy in a lot of trouble. I know I don't have to tell you this, but the information I give you on these things is secret, not for anybody else's ears."

"As always." George nodded and gave the lips-sealed sign.

Chapter 13

LATER THAT DAY GEORGE MET FRIEND RICK at the soda fountain and told him about the Alaska State Trooper coming to his home and lecturing him on honesty, Rick was disbelieving. "I'm glad he didn't come to my house," he said. "My old man would kick my ass."

George tilted his head in a sign of thoughtfulness. "It wasn't that bad," he said. "It did shake me up. The guy made a lot of sense. I've been thinking I might become a lawman. If I had stealing on my record that would be damn near impossible."

Rick laughed. "That wouldn't be a problem for me, especially if I went into politics. I swear people think all politicians are stealing."

"You're kidding," George said. "How can you be in politics and have a criminal record? People would never vote for you."

"Did you ever hear of a guy named Curley?" Rick countered. "James Michael Curley? He was mayor of Boston for a long time. I heard a lot about him when I was in Massachusetts. He held all kinds of political jobs and even got elected to Congress. Curley got busted by the police a couple of times, usually for taking bribes and stuff like that. He went to prison while he was still mayor of Boston and ran the city from his cell. Even when he was in the lockup he did a lot of good things for people, built parks and schools for their kids. Sure, he did a lot of things for his friends and for himself," Rick added. "But there are one heck of a lot of people in Boston, especially the Irish, who got help from Mayor Curley over the years. They loved him for it."

Rick paused to take a breath, his enthusiasm for the subject obvious in his voice. "I know Alaska isn't Boston and you probably couldn't do anything like that here," he said, "but Curley proved that if people are on your side and they don't like the guys who are after you, they'll support you, almost no matter what."

George shook his head and smiled broadly. "That's good to know, my friend, but I think I'll take the high road and keep my nose clean. If you get busted and go to jail, I'll come visit you."

At that point George's girlfriend Cindy entered the soda fountain with Rick's latest girlfriend, Alice Togart. The girls approached their booth. The two boys rose and Rick said: "Hello there. The room has suddenly seemed a brighter place. Please join us and sit down."

As the girls slid into the seats beside their boyfriends, Cindy gave George a questioning look and said: "What have you two been up to. You weren't talking about us behind our backs, were you?"

George started to answer and Rick said: "Not at all. Except in the nicest possible way."

"I'll bet," Cindy said.

Chapter 14

IN HIS SENIOR YEAR AT ANCHORAGE HIGH, George applied for a scholarship at the University of Alaska Fairbanks. Two months later he received a phone call from the university dean's office. "You got it, young man," the caller said. "You have a sharp young mind and have won a full-ride ticket to UAF."

"What does that mean?" George asked.

"All of your classes will be covered at no cost to you. You'll have to pay for housing and meals, but if you're willing to work we can find you a job that should cover those expenses. You are a bright young man and we have great hopes for you. While you are here I hope you'll work hard and fulfill the promise we see in you."

A broad smile crossed George's face. "I will," he said. "I'll work very hard. I promise. I'll try to earn every dollar you spend on me." George thanked the caller profusely, dropped the phone into its cradle and shouted "Yahoo!" He ran into the kitchen to tell his mother, then returned to the phone, dialed Rick's home number and gave him the news.

"Way to go," Rick replied. "UAF is a good school. It looks like I'll be going to Saint Cloud, like my dad."

"Where in hell is that?" George asked.

"Minnesota," Rick answered. "Way far away."

George was saddened by the news. He and Rick had been close throughout their high school years and the thought that their two-man team might go separate ways was unsettling. "You'll come back to Alaska, right?"

"Oh yeah," Rick said. "I'm a lifer. This place is in my blood now."

George's trip to the University of Alaska campus in Fairbanks involved a 360-mile drive from Anchorage. Rick's journey to Minnesota required boarding a steamer for the 1,400- mile sail south from Seward to Seattle followed by a 1,500-mile eastward train trip to Saint Cloud. Before departing, the two young men got together one evening to prepare themselves for the long separation and the new and diverse courses their lives were taking. Rick brought a six-pack of beer, which an older friend bought for him. They shared it in the shade of birch trees in a Downtown Anchorage park.

"Good luck, old buddy," George said. "I hope you come back here after you finish at Saint Cloud."

Rick swallowed a mouthful of beer and said: "Oh, I'll be back. You'll never get rid of me. Alaska is in my blood now. There's no way I could stay away. And I'll be coming back for vacations. My folks are here and it's my home now."

"I look forward to seeing you when you get back," George replied. "I've only had a few close friends in my life, and you are definitely one of them. I've known a lot of people and got along with most of them. But you and I are what I would call teammates."

"I'll drink to that" Rick said, clinking his half-empty beer bottle against the one in George's hand. "Keep your nose clean and you might wind up getting that law enforcement job you want."

George leaned back against the birch tree, closed his eyes and said: "Come back here when you graduate."

"You betcha. And you keep on wooing that Cindy. You've got a keeper there and you don't want to lose her."

George smiled broadly. "I know that—and I will."

Chapter 15

---•---

GEORGE'S FATHER DROVE HIM TO FAIRBANKS for the start of classes in September. He helped the boy negotiate enrollment and finding a room in a dormitory. At the end of the day he took the boy aside and said:

"Son, I'm very proud of you. I don't remember ever saying that before but this is a very special time in your life. While you are at college you won't have your mom or I to give you day to day guidance. I do hope you will call us at least a couple of times a week and make the calls collect. If you want and need it we will give you whatever guidance we can. But for the most part you will be making your own decisions and I hope they will be good ones. UAF is a fine school and one I would have chosen for myself if I could have gone to college. But my family had no money and none of us went beyond high school. You are the first in the family to go so I hope you will work hard and make us proud. When the time comes I hope you'll give a lot of thought to what you want to do for work. A lot of opportunities will be opening for you. If I can give any guidance I'll give it when you call but this is all new to me so I might not be much help. You have it in you to succeed. I know you do. I know you will work hard and do what is expected of you. Good luck."

George's dad threw his arms around his son, hugged him hard and then dropped his arms.

"Thanks Dad," George said as his father turned and walked back toward his car.

THE APPEARANCE OF TROOPER SERGEANT PARKER in George Tallent's bedroom that winter day of his sophomore year in high school impressed the boy tremendously. The sergeant's words stuck with him throughout the balance of his high school career and into his senior year at the University of Alaska. Since his old boss had never made an official report on George's brief experiment with stealing merchandise, the boy had no record and was eligible for police work. When he discussed his thoughts with his parents, they encouraged him to apply for the Alaska Public Safety Training Academy in Sitka after graduating from the university. He did, was accepted and his father put him on a flight from Anchorage to Sitka to begin a sixteen-week program of instruction in criminal investigation, police procedure, laws and physical skills.

While attending the Public Safety Academy, George filled out an application for the Alaska State Troopers. He was interviewed by an officer visiting the campus and two weeks later received a job offer from the state's most prestigious police organization. His appointment was a historic occasion since he was the first Alaska Native to become an Alaska State Trooper, an organization with a long and proud tradition of service to the 49th state.

Governor Ernest Gruening was the featured speaker at the Public Safety Academy graduation. At the close of the ceremonies Gruening made a point of walking over to George on the building's stage and shaking his hand. "Congratulations, young man," he said. "Let's hope you are the first of many."

Rick stayed in class politics throughout his high school years, went on to Saint Cloud and graduated with a degree in logistics in June of 1964. When he returned to Anchorage he became aware of growing excitement about the continuing oil development in Cook Inlet, where companies were then building offshore drilling platforms. The platform construction began several years after

Richfield's historic discovery on the Kenai Peninsula in 1957 while the two boys were in high school. They were barely aware of the discovery at the time but Alaska's economy had thrived as a result of it and Anchorage took on the distinctive flare of a boomtown with busy nightclubs and a thriving commercial district. The earlier onshore discovery led to exploration of rock reservoirs lying deep beneath the inlet itself and the platforms above were built to produce the oil and ship it to a tanker loading facility under construction nearby.

After their graduations George went to work as an Alaska State Trooper and Rick took a job in the supply operation supporting a Cook Inlet drilling firm. It was a relatively low-level position but it paid well. George and Cindy resumed dating after he was assigned to an Alaska State Trooper position in the Matanuska Valley north of Anchorage. Rick went through a series of girlfriends as was his custom.

Chapter 16

———•———

IN DECEMBER OF 1967 THE ANCHORAGE TIMES carried a short item reporting that bush pilots on Alaska's North Slope were seeing gas flaring at a wildcat drill site operated by Richfield Oil Corporation at the mouth of the Sagavanirktok, a wide Arctic river with an Alaska Eskimo name. The Sag River, as it was commonly called, flows north from the edge of the Brooks Mountain Range to the Arctic Ocean near Prudhoe Bay, 700 miles north of Anchorage. The site was several hundred miles east of the nearest known oil field south of Barrow and in the calving grounds of a caribou herd consisting of 200,000 animals.

In March, the company announced that it had made a major discovery at the Prudhoe Bay site. The initial estimate was that the field contained about 9.6 billion barrels of recoverable oil and 26 trillion cubic feet of gas. If the estimates proved accurate, the field would be the largest ever discovered in North America. Excitement grew rapidly throughout the state and Rick Albert applied for a job. The Richfield recruiter offered him a position as a materials man. His job was keeping the rig crew supplied with whatever the men needed, including aircraft. The position was a mid-level assignment that came with an attractive salary and firm guidance on an important matter. All company crews operating in a remote area like Prudhoe Bay were to fly in charter aircraft, each with two engines and two pilots. No exceptions. Company officials considered it an important safety matter, especially in a remote operating area like Prudhoe Bay.

The twin-engine charters were expensive, more than double the cost of some single-engine aircraft, so young Rick soon decided that the company didn't mind spending money. He also found he could make cash on the side by suggesting to charter aircraft operators that contracts could be decided in their favor if they met all safety criteria and paid him a little something in cash. It wasn't much; he didn't dare take more than a few hundred dollars at a time, but it supplemented his already sizable paycheck. Rick considered the extra money a gratuity in payment for his prompt attention to bidding matters.

One morning early in his career Rick accompanied a visiting team of heavy equipment vendors on a flight to a remote drilling site near Prudhoe Bay. The loading facility and transportation system were yet to be built and the company's owners were lobbying heavily for the right to extend a pipeline across millions of acres of public land. Environmental activists in what Alaskans call The Lower 48 fought them at every turn and lobbied Congress to block construction of the 800-mile pipeline. They argued that such development would be a disaster for wildlife, especially the 200,000 caribou that made up the Porcupine herd, named for the nearby Porcupine River.

RICK ALBERT'S DRILLING RIG WAS POSITIONED ON A GRAVEL PAD five miles from the shore of the vast, deeply frozen Arctic Ocean. Visits to the site always involved a stop at the company's dock, where ships brought supplies during the summer when the near-shore ice was always melted.

Standing on the long causeway leading to the dock it occurred to Rick that if a man were able to travel over the sea ice, he could easily reach Russia and with a bit more exertion could get to Greenland and take a ship south to the East Coast of the United

States thousands of miles from Alaska. He and the crew were very much at the top of the world, a place with a unique perspective and a weird and unprecedented feeling of superiority to the mere mortals who occupied the planet's more southern regions.

"Is that a polar bear?" one man asked.

"It is indeed," Rick replied. "I wonder what he's doing so near shore. They usually stay in deeper water where the seals are."

"He's got something in his mouth," the man noted.

Rick smiled and clapped his hands together. "He does indeed. And it looks like a seal. We are in luck. The seals must have chased the bait fish into this cove. Keep your eyes open. No telling what might be here today."

The group watched intently until Rick decided it was time to head for the airport and their rendezvous with the flight crew. "Everybody onto the bus," he called. "The show here seems to be over and we should head back."

His visitors replied with good-natured grumbling and walked back to the waiting bus. The driver swung open the door and smiled as his passengers filed aboard and took their seats.

"Let's work our way to the airport," Rick told the man. "It's time to head south. But I'd like to stop off and visit our drilling rig along the way, show these folks what it's all about here."

As the last visitor filed aboard, the driver gave the thumbs-up sign, closed the bus door and turned his bus south to the airport.

When they approached the drilling rig, their guide invited them to exit the bus and climb to a rig floor where a foreman was directing a four-man crew busily swinging huge gripping devices. The oversized wrenches were tightly closed on a long portion of pipe six inches wide and twenty-seven feet long connected to a series of pipes extending into the tundra beneath the rig floor.

"Get them tongs back, boys," the foreman shouted over the noise from the rig's massive engine. "Get 'em back."

The workers, bare-armed despite a wintry breeze sweeping through the rig's superstructure, yanked on chains attached to the three-foot wrenches.

Rick gathered his visiting vendors into a small circle at the edge of the rig floor. The company guide stood back while Rick spoke to the visitors.

"Those tongs are very large wrenches," he said, "and the pipes you can see running through the rig floor are attached to a long string of connected pipe that right now probably extend about two thousand feet through the permafrost. The oil formation it's drilling toward is about eight thousand feet below our boots. It will take a week or more for the drill bit to reach the oil," he added, "but once it does the drill pipe will be extended deep into the formation and attached to a conductor to carry the oil to the surface. From here it will be carried to a line to carry it to the Trans-Alaska Pipeline and then on to a tanker terminal in Valdez on the Gulf of Alaska. A tanker ship will carry it by sea to the Lower 48, possibly a port in northern California."

"Doesn't the oil freeze?" one of the visitors asked. He knew that the air temperature outside the rig was somewhere near forty below zero.

"No," Rick answered with a laugh. "The temperature of the oil in the ground is somewhere over two hundred degrees. The pipe and pipeline are insulated to keep the oil in and fluid enough to be pumped."

"That's not what we hear from the environmentalists," one of the equipment vendors said.

Rick grimaced. The green zealots had become mortal enemies of the oil drillers. Few had ever been north of the Arctic Circle and most knew little about oil drilling but that didn't stop them from demonstrating against the petroleum companies in the larger communities of Anchorage and Fairbanks and outside Richfield's corporate headquarters in Los Angeles.

Chapter 17

———◆———

IN LATE AFTERNOON RICK LED HIS VISITORS ABOARD his company's Lear Jet, got them seated and belted in. One of the two pilots came back to check on them, then returned to his seat in the cockpit.

After the Lear took off from the Prudhoe Bay airfield and climbed out of the basin as they approached the Brooks Mountain Range, Rick opened a panel in the wall beside him. Behind it was a well-stocked mini-bar. "Can I interest anyone in a libation?" he asked. All six of the visitors took him up on the offer and the balance of the trip was taken up with questions raised from their time on the Arctic tundra. Rick knew the answers to most of their questions and promised to research the few that he couldn't answer.

ONE MORNING IN LATE JANUARY, Rick drove into the Richfield parking lot, waved to the security guard and walked past him to the building's elevator. When he neared his office he noticed that all of his colleagues were engaged in intense telephone conversations. His supervisor, George Pruitt, held up a hand that urgently suggested he approach.

"What's up?" Rick asked.

Pruitt placed a hand over his phone's speaker. "Have you been listening to the news?" he asked.

"No. Nothing bad about our company, I hope."

"Not us," Pruitt said. "Union Oil. A bad blowout at a drilling rig in Southern California. Someplace near Santa Barbara, in the channel that runs near the city. They have a bunch of platforms in the water there. This is going to be bad news for the whole industry, I'm afraid."

"Wow," Rick said as he moved quickly to the office teletype, which was then relaying news items about a major oil spill then darkening the sea in the Santa Barbara Channel. It was an uncontrolled blowout that the experts estimated would be difficult to contain.

From a window behind his deck Rick could see crowds beginning to form on the sidewalk outside. They included a preponderance of young people and their growing numbers were already spreading into the street and blocking traffic.

"Walt," he shouted to Pruitt. "We are going to need all the security we can locate. I would suggest we call in all off-duty personnel and also contact the city police. This could easily get out of hand. Some of those people are looking pretty angry and they are already starting to chant."

Rick recoiled reflexively as a rock smashed the window in front of him. "Everybody get down," he shouted.

Moments later a half-dozen security people rushed into the room, pulled down the window shades and closed the drapes.

"Everybody, please stay where they are!" the security chief shouted. "The city police will be clearing the sidewalk outside in a few minutes. Until they arrive, I don't want anyone making themselves a target."

Rick turned on the office radio and tuned it to an all-news channel that was then broadcasting from a California studio which was trying to connect with a telephone booth close to the spill site. The results were sporadic.

"I'm going to have to break off this call for the time being," the reporter said, an angry tone to his voice. "The police are trying to move us back away from the blowout. Apparently there is a severe fire danger." In the background could be heard a cacophony of shouted questions.

The next few hours were consumed by a flood of news from Santa Barbara, all of it bad except for sporadic descriptions of the recovery efforts being made by the oil workers. Rick sent two office workers to a nearby restaurant with orders to bring back as much prepared food as they could find. He asked the staff to call family members and warn them they might not be home that night.

Rick tried to nap on the office couch after midnight but his frayed nerves and the unrelenting bad news from California made sleep impossible. The spill and the battle to contain it went on for a week and the massive cleanup would require months. Before it ended many of the company's office workers—as well as field staff—were beginning to rethink their career trajectories.

The next morning he awoke to shouting from the street outside. One young man carried a sign that said in large letters: "Get Oil Out of Alaska!"

Behind him strode another young man with a sign that said: "No Santa Barbara's in Alaska!!"

There were about fifty marchers in all and their faces and strutting suggested they were angry. One stooped to pick up a rock, spotted a security guard taking his picture and dropped the rock.

When the phone rang he picked it up to hear his supervisor's voice once again. "Things are still going downhill in California," he said. "And it's looking like the wild ones in Alaska will be on our back for months, at least. Get the building secured and tell the staff to settle down for a long haul."

Chapter 18

———·———

PRUITT'S PREDICTION PROVED TO BE CORRECT. The demonstrations continued and went on daily for the following two weeks. Rick thought to himself that the heated opposition to oil operations was likely to be permanent. Many people were drawn to Alaska for its beautiful scenery and abundant fish and wildlife, all of which appeared to be threatened by drilling and other oilfield operations. He prayed quietly that all of his people would be very careful. A major oil spill would destroy his company's reputation and jeopardize its continued operations.

Fortunately the following months in Alaska were uneventful.

One morning later that year Pruitt, met him at the door of his Anchorage office. Rick unlocked the door and waved Pruitt to an overstuffed chair and asked: "What's up? You have a serious look on your face."

Pruitt rubbed his hands together, leaned forward and said: "You are aware that Humble Oil is moving a tanker from New Jersey through the ice fields in the Northwest Passage to Alaska, I'm sure."

Rick laughed. "Are you kidding? It's been all over the news. Do we have an arrival date yet?"

"September 20," Pruitt said. "There will be a bunch of dignitaries at Prudhoe to welcome the crews of the ship and the Coast Guard icebreaker that's leading the way. Humble is testing the feasibility of moving North Slope oil through the Arctic Ocean to the East Coast. The tanker has a reinforced hull and is one of a kind. Humble wants Richfield to send someone like you to go along and do whatever needs to be done to support the operation."

Rick had an unbelieving look on his face. "They're not going to dock that tanker at Prudhoe, are they?"

"No," Pruitt replied, "that wouldn't be possible. The water is too shallow for a large ship and stays shallow a long way out. The tanker will probably hold about twenty miles offshore, wherever the captain decides to stop. The tanker has a helipad so I assume people will use a chopper to get back and forth. Let me know what you need. I gave your phone number to Humble's Alaska manager, Phil Ferguson, but you might want to give him a call." Pruitt handed Rick a business card with the man's phone number and an embossed emblem of the huge oil company.

When Pruitt walked out of his office Rick called the number for the Humble manager. The man's secretary answered. "Mr. Ferguson is very busy," she said. "Can I tell him what this is about."

Rick explained his role at Richfield's Alaska office and offered to provide any logistical support needed by the arrival of the tanker Manhattan.

"I can probably help you with that," she said. "It's quite likely that I'll be liaison between you and Mr. Ferguson. I'll make a list of what we need and get it to you."

Rick spent four days at his office doing a paper inventory of supplies on hand in Richfield's Anchorage warehouse but never heard back from the Humble Oil manager's secretary. He resumed his duties, which involved spending about half his time running errands around the city and half at the warehouse and his office.

On September 19, a day before the expected arrival of the tanker Manhattan and its Coast Guard icebreaker escort, Pruitt notified Tallent that management wanted a symbolic barrel of oil delivered to the Manhattan while it waited off Prudhoe Bay. It was to be the culmination of the tanker's 5,000-mile trip from New Jersey and crossing the frozen Arctic Ocean and would give the Manhattan some oil to take back to the East Coast. If the trip were deemed a success it would open the way for shipment of North Slope oil to the U.S. East Coast and Europe. Otherwise the oil's distribution would be limited to the sizable but more limited market around the Pacific Ocean.

"Where do I get a barrel container?" Rick asked. "I don't think there is any such thing."

Pruitt nodded. A barrel was a measurement of oil, 42 gallons. The closest container in reality was the ubiquitous 55-gallon drum, which once had littered the North Slope landscape from the early years of oil exploration. When Richfield first became active at Prudhoe, cleaning up and removing the oil drums had been a major requirement to demonstrate its environmental citizenship.

All of the oil drums then in use on the North Slope were shipped there by a single supplier in Anchorage and all notably bore the logo of Chevron Oil, one of Humble's competitors.

"You'll have to get it painted," Pruitt said while clapping his hands.

"What color?" Rick asked.

The supervisor mulled the question briefly, then smiled, rubbed his hands together and said proudly: "Gold."

Rick thought to himself *Good Lord* but didn't say the words aloud.

The decision on the barrel's paint job seemed to make sense to Pruitt so Rick asked the company's logistics department to make it happen and to fill the barrel with North Slope oil. The next day, after the flight from Anchorage to Prudhoe Bay, Rick and his company colleagues were mingling with the dignitaries when a truck rumbled up to the edge of the helipad and a crew began work to load up the symbolic golden barrel. As a workman removed a canvas covering and began strapping the barrel into its harness, Rick stared at it in horror.

The barrel had the usual dings and dents of any well-used North Slope barrel and the gilt paint emphasized its imperfections, making it one of the ugliest sights Tallent had ever seen. To his enormous relief, the visitors pretended the barrel was the most beautiful thing *they* had ever seen. The visitors, including the half dozen news reporters among them, were taken by the symbolism of the golden barrel more than its unmistakable ugliness. All pretended it was indeed a beautiful sight though all could almost certainly appreciate its awful appearance.

"Oh my god," Tallent whispered to himself.

"What did you say?" Pruitt asked from his side.

"Nothing," he replied. "I think everybody likes it."

The "golden barrel," as it was called, was paraded in front of the assembled dignitaries, reporters and photographers. Though Rick would open the Anchorage newspaper next day with great trepidation, the dents were not noticeable in the photographs and the writer pretended it was a wonderful sight to see. So did every other person covering the story and Rick's reputation was actually enhanced by the day's drama. The crowd was so pleased to be present for the historic occasion that the praise for Rick's ugly bucket was universal.

As the helicopter lifted off to deliver the golden barrel to the Manhattan, a tall and rather thin man approached and extended his hand. "Rick Albert, I'm Hank Rosenthal. I came up on the tanker and will be staying to handle public relations for Humble Oil in Alaska."

Rick shook the man's hand and said: "Welcome to Alaska, Hank Rosenthal. It must have been an interesting trip coming through that ice."

"Oh yeah," Rosenthal said. "It certainly was, but there were many surprises. I expected to see a lot of critters but other than a few polar bears and some wandering seagulls we didn't see much of anything. I've always heard Alaska was full of fish and game."

"Oh it really is," Rick said. "There are a lot of fish in the Arctic Ocean along with a bunch of whales and sea creatures, but I'm not surprised you didn't see many from that icebreaking tanker. The ship and the Coast Guard cutter that accompanied it make way too much noise with your engines and grinding through the ice. Probably scared critters for miles around. Are you a hunter or fisherman?"

A wide smile crossed Rosenthal's face. "I sure am," he said. "I enjoy both and am looking forward to getting out and trying everything while I'm in Alaska. I expect to be here for a long time, maybe forever."

The man made a surprisingly strong impression on Rick Albert. If this guy wants to go hunting and fishing, he thought, he has come to the right place. "I'd be glad to take you out and show you a few things," he said. "Here, take my card and give me a call when you get settled."

"Will do," Rosenthal said.

As Rick took his card a nearby group of news reporters became aware of Rosenthal's presence, crowded around him and opened a cascade of questions about the historic voyage.

"Call me," Rick shouted over their heads.

A smiling Rosenthal waved to him before turning to the surrounding reporters and inviting them to direct their questions to him. The reporters all seemed to be asking at the same time with little deference to each other. Rosenthal laughed and pointed to one reporter in an unspoken invitation to ask the first question. The others clamored but settled down as Rosenthal answered the first.

Chapter 19

———•———

T WO DAYS LATER RICK'S PHONE RANG. "Rick, it's Hank Rosenthal. We met when the Manhattan arrived at Prudhoe Bay."

Rick laughed. "Well, hello there, Hank Rosenthal. I didn't expect to hear from you so soon. How can I be of help?"

"I'd like to take you up on your offer of getting out to enjoy Alaska," he replied. "Right now I have some free time after that trip. I don't expect it to last so I'd like to take you up on your offer while I can. Seems like there should be some good fishing at this time of year."

"There is indeed," Rick said. "The silver salmon are running in the rivers right now. They are fun to catch, very powerful and put up a heck of a struggle. And they are very good to eat."

"Sounds good," Rosenthal replied. "When can you get away?"

"Would tomorrow be too soon?" Rick asked. "I'm dying to get out of this office."

"Tomorrow would be perfect. I'm staying at the Captain Cook Hotel. Can you pick me up there?"

"I can indeed," Rick said. "I'll pick you up at 7 a.m. High tide at the river mouth is at 9:30. We'll have a couple of hours of rising tide, the best time for these salmon."

"Great," Rosenthal replied. "I don't have any fishing gear. None of my stuff would be of much use here. Could you loan me a few things? If anything gets broken I promise to replace it."

"I'd be glad to loan you some equipment. See you in the morning."

RICK PULLED INTO THE HOTEL GATEWAY DRIVE shortly before 7 and found Hank Rosenthal waiting by the door. He wore outdoor clothing and hip-boots but didn't appear to have any fishing gear whatever. Rick was not surprised; few visitors were equipped for Alaska salmon fishing unless they were planning on it.

Hank opened the door of Rick's 20-year-old Volvo, shook Rick's hand and sat smiling as they drove away from the hotel.

"Good morning, Hank," Rick said. "Let's get on the road."

"One nice thing I already like about fishing in Alaska," Rosenthal said, "is that you don't have to get out of bed at a ridiculous hour like you do chasing trout in the rivers of Montana."

Rick laughed. "That's true, sometimes. The best fishing is on the incoming tide and that depends more on the moon than anything. When the tide is going out the salmon don't generally fight it. The best fishing depends on a lot of things, including what they are feeding on. We also have some nice trout and they sometimes occupy the same waters. I was thinking we might try a little no-name creek in the Matanuska Valley north of here. At this time of year we are likely to encounter trout or salmon. And we can fish with them using fly rods, my favorite way. When you are casting flies in this river you might catch just about anything."

"I like the way you think," Rosenthal said. "I'm surprised we aren't going to be using a boat."

"Actually," Rick replied, "that is the way most people fish for salmon. They troll lures from a boat, sometimes in fresh water, sometimes in salt water. If you are going to be around Anchorage for a while, we can give that a try as well."

"Sounds good to me. I've been fly fishing in Montana and got a big kick out of it. And I'm hoping I get to spend years in Alaska, as long as Humble Oil lets me." Rosenthal winked and added: "And who knows, maybe even if it doesn't."

The drive to the river took less than an hour but it gave the two men a better chance to get acquainted. When they arrived at a highway turnoff Rick pulled his car in and parked, then lifted his rear hatch to show Rosenthal the equipment they would be using. When Rick handed Hank an aluminum tube, Rosenthal knew exactly what it was, opened the end and gently removed an aged bamboo rod. He skillfully strung the line and leader, then tied on a bushy fly with hook.

"This is obviously not your first fishing trip," Rick noted, obviously impressed by his skill with equipment. He nodded and led Hank down a trail to the small river. When they arrived, Rick pointed silently toward the center of the river, where a school of Alaska silver salmon were splashing as they fed on a school of minnows.

Both men began wading at the edge of the river and were soon busily engaged in catching the fish. Rick dispatched his first fish with a small rock to limit its suffering, then released his second fish to resume its journey.

Hank waded closer to Rick and was about to ask a question when Rick said: "These fish are delicious and even one is more than my wife and I can eat, so I like to keep the first salmon I catch and then switch to catch and release. If the trout are biting, and they might, I release all of those that I catch. A trout is a beautiful thing and I just can't bring myself to killing one of those. Salmon die after they spawn but trout can live for years."

Hank nodded his agreement and said: "My wife won't arrive here from Houston for another week or so. She has to close out our place there before she comes to Anchorage."

"Well then," Rick replied, "please join my wife and I this evening. I'll be cooking this salmon on my grill and we can tell you everything we know about Alaska and how to survive here."

"I would be delighted to join you," Hank said. "Your hospitality and kindness to this Texas newcomer are most welcome. By the way," he added, "Is this really a no-name creek?"

"The locals call it Fish Creek," he said. "For obvious reasons. But the maps have no name for it. There are a lot of creeks and

lakes in Alaska. It's a huge place and the mapmakers haven't gotten
around to naming all the water."

"Fish Creek it is," Rosenthal answered.

Chapter 20

RICK WAS POPULAR WITH BOTH MEN AND WOMEN, and when he later went into politics his charm would enable him to win votes from both sexes. In the meantime it frequently provided opportunities for sexual adventures with the friendlier ones. While still working for the oil company, he dated many of the most attractive of the young women in Anchorage, switching from one to another every few months.

The oilpatch job paid well but required being away from the city for weeks at a time, a distinct disadvantage to his interests both in romance and the urban life. He had a degree in education from Saint Cloud University and a master's degree in school administration from the University of Minnesota.

His education and work experience qualified him for many jobs, including some that paid well and allowed him to spend the bulk of his time in Anchorage. After he managed to put several thousand dollars away in a bank, Rick applied for and was offered a job as a guidance counselor in the Anchorage school district, including his alma mater, Anchorage High.

One morning Rick was surprised to see his old friend George waiting outside his office door when Rick arrived just before eight a.m. George was in civilian clothes, leaving his trooper uniform at home to avoid calling attention to the unannounced and unexpected visit to the guidance counselor's office.

"Good, morning, George," he said jovially. "Come on in. To what do I owe the pleasure? I assume this is not an official visit."

George hesitated awkwardly, obviously embarrassed. "Thanks, Rick. No, this time I'm here on a family matter. My young cousin Rodney Crockett is a freshman here at the high school and has been getting into a little trouble. I offered to talk to you about it."

"Police business kind of trouble?"

"No," George replied. "Not yet anyway. I want him to straighten himself out before he does get in a jam. If he did, it would presumably be with the Anchorage city police rather than the State Troopers. But if he doesn't keep his nose clean the family is going to send him back to live with relatives in the village. They are embarrassed about his behavior."

Rick had a surprised look on his face. "I've met Rodney and was impressed by him. He has a few rough edges but you expect that when a boy is trying to adjust to city life after being brought up in a village. What has he been up to?"

"We're not sure, exactly," George answered. "His parents think he is smoking marijuana. And he has been coming home with a lot of stuff that we know he didn't have the money to buy."

Rick laughed. "That sounds familiar. Could it be a little money-making scheme like the one you and I got into trouble for?"

"It could be something like that," George answered. "At least we think so. Right now I'm most concerned about the kids he is hanging around with in school. He's lost interest in his studies. I'm not sure about marijuana but I know he smokes cigarettes behind the classroom building and spends a lot of time around the five-and-dime store where the tough kids hang out."

"I'll be glad to talk to him," Rick offered. "I might be able to get him interested in school, especially if he's willing to talk about what he likes and dislikes about it. He seems to be a fine young man with a lot of potential. He needs to be thinking about how he might use that to build a life for himself."

"I agree," George said. As he left the building it occurred to the young trooper that his nephew was in a situation similar to the one he himself faced when Sergeant Walter Parker came to his home. The boy needed a role model to replace those he left behind when his family moved from remote Kiana to Anchorage.

Rick drove to the home of George's sister, walked up and rapped on the door. He removed his cap and said: "Hello, I'm Rick Albert, guidance counselor at Anchorage High School. George told me you were having problems with your boy Rodney. It sounds like it might be getting a little more than kid stuff," he said. "I think I might be able to help and would like to talk to him before it gets serious."

"George told me you might be coming by," Marilyn said. "Please talk to him and see what you think," Marilyn said. "He doesn't seem to hear anything I say to him. But I know he really looks up to you and George both. His room is at the top of the stairs."

"I'll be glad to give it a try," he said as he headed up the stairs. At the top of the stairs he rapped on the boy's door.

The door opened slowly and a timid boy peaked out. "Can I come in?" Rick asked.

The boy had a quizzical look on his face and swung the door wide. "Sure," he said. "Any time."

Rick took a seat next to the armchair where Rodney did much of his studying.

"Am I in trouble?" the boy asked

"Not that I know of," Rick said. "But I wanted to talk a bit and make sure you aren't heading in the wrong direction."

Rodney nodded. "What have you heard about me?"

"I hear you've been smoking cigarettes, skipping a few classes, hanging out with a tough crowd and have been seen with merchandise that didn't belong to you."

The boy's eyes went wide. "Some of that stuff is true," he said, "but I'm just doing what everybody else is doing."

"I've talked to your teachers," Rick responded. "They are worried about you. They really like you and want you to succeed. I'll be glad to do whatever I can to help. If necessary I could even arrange to have you transferred to another school. You could go to East High. That's a little further away but we could provide transportation. That would get you away from the temptations at Anchorage."

Tears streamed down Rodney's face. "Oh please, don't do that," he said. "I want to stay at Anchorage High. I can get clean and would like to make some new friends. Most of the guys I have been hanging with are getting to be a bit too much. They get me in a lot of trouble, even in the neighborhood."

"OK then," Rick countered. "Let's give it another try. If you stay away from the cigarettes, quit skipping classes and make some new friends we'll let you remain at Anchorage. But if it doesn't work out, East High will be on the table."

"Thank you, thank you," the boy said, his hands in a prayerful position. "I'll start on it tomorrow morning."

Rick wished Rodney good luck, left the room and nodded smiling to his mother as he passed her on his way out the door. The woman smiled and mouthed the words: "Thank you."

That summer George bought a second-hand outboard motor for his boat and spent the next three weekends with the boy trolling for salmon on the Kenai River. Young Rodney responded well and bragged about how well he was doing in his high school studies and the jobs he intended to pursue after graduation. George decided that he and his nephew would spend every weekend possible on the river.

Chapter 21

⸻

BY LATE FEBRUARY THE CITY OF ANCHORAGE and its sur-roundings would begin to emerge from their long winter. On December 21 the sun is above the horizon only for five and a half hours. By the end of February the amount of potential sunshine—in the absence of clouds—virtually doubles. And given an hour or so of twilight at each end of the day, the sun regains dominance over that part of the world. Night has been vanquished, not to return until the dark days of the following winter. The gloom of midwinter is starting to lift.

Earlier in the winter, the time of the first snow in October, the advancing darkness dominates the city. When snow finally falls and the air is cold enough to allow it to stick to the ground, the white snow actually reflects and magnifies whatever sunlight is available. That brightens the city considerably and has a near magical impact on people's attitudes. The light tends to improve individual out-looks and can relieve marital tensions, with the same impact on the behavior of children. The brighter days of February are often cold but the advancing light of the lengthening days provides yet another uplift to the entire city.

George Tallent was generally a cheerful man. Despite the

downbeat nature of many criminal investigations, he managed to remain upbeat and greeted each day with the optimism of a man who welcomed challenges.

One February day he returned to Alaska State Trooper head-quarters to find a note on his desk asking him to drop by the office of Lieutenant Walter Gilmour, one of the state's best-known police officials.

George rapped on Gilmour's door and when the lieutenant waved at him to come in, the young Trooper stepped inside and took a seat opposite Gilmour's desk. The lieutenant was just finishing up a conversation with someone whom he obviously respected.

Gilmour hung up the phone and turned to George with a forced smile. "Good Morning, Tallent. Thanks for coming by."

"Glad to see you, Lieutenant. Something I can help you with?"

"Yes, that was my buddy John Somerville on the phone. He is the guy I wanted to see you about."

Trooper Tallent's eyes went wide. "Is that Dr. John Somerville, the ophthalmologist?"

"That's him. John is having a problem with his wife Alicia. She has gone missing."

"Do you know much about the circumstances?"

"Some," the major said. "It's a complicated case. His wife is a dancer at The Bush Company."

George had never been there but he knew a lot about The Great Alaska Bush Company. It was a notorious strip club and its name was derived both from the Alaska notion of "the Bush" as wild country and the slang expression for a woman's genital area.

"Wow, a doctor's wife is a dancer at The Bush Company? Is that where he met her?"

"No, they met in college when they were both at the University of Alaska in Fairbanks. He was in pre-med and she was an English major. She and a girlfriend started dancing at a strip club near the campus. Alicia got a big kick out of it and made a lot of money. She is a very pretty woman with a great figure. Guys would give her big tips just for stopping by to talk to them. Some men would give her hundred-dollar tips. Some nights she cleared two thousand bucks."

NORTH COUNTRY DETECTIVE   63

"Did she keep on stripping after college?"

"No," Gilmour replied. "She actually got a job at the city clerk's office. She was bored to tears, no surprise. But she stuck with it while John went to medical school. They got married when he got back and was starting up his ophthalmology practice. Then they found out she couldn't have kids and things got complicated."

"How so?" George asked.

"She decided she wanted to get a little more of the exciting life and went back to dancing at The Bush Company a couple of nights a week. John was very unhappy about it but he worried that not being able to have kids and being bored could drive her over the edge. She liked to drink and he was afraid she might overdo that to the point where it could affect her health or get her into trouble. He was embarrassed about the dancing routine but figured his friends were unlikely to go there. Even if they did, he felt they were unlikely to recognize her and would never make the connection with him."

"Isn't that a little unusual, for a respectable woman to dance in a strip club?"

Gilmour grimaced. "Not as unusual as you might think. Some of the dancers are wild women with ties to the underworld. But some are just local ladies who enjoy the nightlife and the extra money. You might be surprised how often the dancers are just bored military wives or women who hate desk jobs."

"And now your buddy's wife has gone missing?"

"Yes," Gilmour replied. "He is thinking she might have met a guy and run off with him. They haven't been getting along that well lately, in part because of the dancing. But she gets a sexual charge from the whole environment and she might just have met somebody she liked better than John. She might be in an apartment somewhere else in town or even in Seattle."

"Did she take any of her personal items from their house?"

"John can't tell. She left a lot of stuff at the house, but she also kept quite a bit in a locker at The Bush. He really has no idea what she might have with her. He is in a real bind because if word got out about where she works, that could affect his medical practice.

But she is his whole world and he really wants to find out what happened to her, make sure she is safe—*if* she is safe."

George scratched his chin pensively. "Any thoughts on how to begin?"

"I was thinking you and I should go to The Bush Company and see if we can talk to a few of her co-workers."

"In an official capacity?"

"No," Gilmour replied. "If Alicia is in danger—and she could be—we need to find that out and get help to her as soon as we can. But we also need to keep this thing quiet for as long as possible. It could blow up on us and I don't want John to get hurt."

George laughed. "This will be my first visit to a strip club."

"Consider it research," Gilmour said with a smile. "Just part of the job. But, please, wear your civvies. We'll want to have a few drinks and don't want to scandalize the place—or have it empty out."

Chapter 22

THAT NIGHT THE TWO STATE TROOPERS swapped their uniforms for comfortable civilian clothes and made their way to a small table in The Bush Company just after ten p.m. They chose the late hour since that was normally when things got busy at the club. They wanted to experience it when some of the place's regular clientele were present.

Gilmour nodded to a woman who made her way to their table. "George Tallent, this is Julia Damarell," he said. "Julia, this is George, one of the guys I work with."

"Hello, there, George," Julia said. "Do you want the whole routine?"

"No," Gilmour laughed. "You can keep your clothes on. I was just hoping you might be able to tell us a little more about Alicia Somerville and where you think she might be these days."

As Julia started to speak she noticed George was staring intensely at the staircase leading from the floor above. Just starting to walk down was a scantily-clad woman, one of the most gorgeous creatures the young Trooper had ever seen.

"That's Amelia," Julia said. "She is one of our newest dancers, just hired the other day. We've hired a lot of new ones in the last few months and she is one of the most popular. Lots of turnover lately. I'll be glad to introduce her to you if you like."

George shook his head. "Thank you. That is an interesting thought but I'm technically still working and I need to keep my mind on the job."

Gilmour was smiling broadly. "Well, Tallent, I'm glad to hear you still have your mind on work, even in the face of such delightful temptation. I should have warned you about what things might be like here but I assumed that a young guy like you would be well-informed about The Bush Company, perhaps even a customer."

"Not me, Lieutenant," George said sheepishly. "Sorry about the distraction. I do need to get out more."

Gilmour gave George an intense look that suggested he avoid using titles unless absolutely necessary.

"Back to business," Gilmour said. "Julia, tell us whatever you can about Alicia Somerville. When did you last see her and where do you think she is now?"

George turned back to Julia, whose attire was every bit as revealing as that of the woman on the stairway above, but Julia seemed more intense and focused on what she saw as a problem. She was obviously very worried.

"Well gentlemen," she said. "The doctor's wife has been dancing here two nights a week for the last couple of months. She has always been punctual and doesn't go on dates with customers that I know of. She's married, which few dancers are. I know she and her husband have been having some difficulty but nothing that unusual for gals who work here. Some of them have roving eyes just like the guys who come here for drinks and kinks, as I like to say."

Gilmour nodded. "When was the last time she came to work? "

"I think it was about three weeks ago. Yeah, three weeks."

"Did she leave anything here?"

"Not that I know of. She has a few dance costumes in a locker but that's about it. Nobody trusts anybody very much in this racket so they don't leave valuables where they might get stolen."

As they talked, Gilmour's eyes scanned the room and he noticed a man approaching the bar, a man whose face looked vaguely familiar.

"Excuse me, Julia, do you know that guy standing in front of the bartender."

"Oh yeah," she said. "That's Phineas Barker, one of our regulars."

"Do you know anything about him?"

"He cooks in a small restaurant in the Spenard neighborhood. He comes here a lot after his place closes for the night. Big tipper so I think he must have another way of making money than managing a Spenard food joint. And he flies an airplane, one of the small ones that can land in tight places."

Gilmour asked: "Does he own the restaurant by any chance?"

"He could," she said. "That would explain a lot of things."

"Such as?"

"Well, he drives a new pickup truck, a nice one. I know that because he damn near ran me over when he was pulling out of the parking lot last week."

"Was anyone in the truck with him?"

"There could have been," she replied. "I couldn't see the passenger side of the truck. I was too busy getting out of the way."

Chapter 23

———•———

A S THEY LEFT THE CLUB LATER THAT EVENING, Gilmour told George: "Find out what you can about that Phineas Barker. I have his name listed in my asshole book and I'd like to know more."

George nodded and made a mental note. Gilmour's "asshole book" was an informal list the lieutenant kept of people to look to when problems arose in the community. The individuals lived on the margins of society and were frequent trouble-makers.

The next afternoon, George had a doctor's appointment. He had called that morning and requested an interview with Dr. John Somerville, the ophthalmologist whose wife was missing. At 2 p.m. he arrived at Somerville's office and was invited into a back office.

"Doctor Somerville," he said after shaking the man's hand, "I'm sorry to hear that your wife is missing. Do you have any idea where she might be? I was wondering if there had been any changes in her life lately that might suggest her whereabouts?"

The ophthalmologist grimaced and wrung his hands. "I wish I could," he said. "This is very unlike her. I was afraid something like this might happen when she started dancing again. It's no job for a doctor's wife. Dancers meet some very strange men. And you never can tell when one of them might be dangerous."

"Why do you say that?" Tallent asked. "Did you have somebody in mind in that regard?"

"No," Dr. Somerville replied. "I think it just goes with the job. Those strip clubs attract a lot of good men, I suspect, but they also draw a few creeps. I asked Amelia many times to quit that damn job, but she didn't want to. She enjoys the place and I suspect she enjoys showing off her body to men. She has a great figure and I know she is proud of it."

"Did she ever mention anyone in particular?"

"No," he said, "not that I recall. The only people she ever mentioned to me were the women she worked with, her fellow dancers."

"Do you have any of those names?"

"Just one," the doctor replied. "She was friends with a woman named Cynthia Wooden. They started work at about the same time and they spent a lot of their spare time together."

"Anything else come to mind that might be useful?" George asked.

"No," Dr. Somerville said. "I can't think of anything."

George gave the doctor his business card and asked him to call if he happened to recall anything his wife might have mentioned about her job, the people she worked with or the men she met at the club.

THE NEXT DAY GEORGE STARTED HIS FORMAL RESEARCH on Phineas Barker. The man was something of an enigma. He was an Alaska sportsman, a hunter and the pilot of a light plane, a SuperCub he owned and housed in a hangar at Anchorage's Merrill Field. Barker's plane was a popular model often flown by sportsmen. It had oversized tundra tires and could be flown in and out of wild country by landing on beaches and in open and grassy fields.

Barker had done time in prison, a brief stay for roughing up a prostitute. He also had friends including several noteworthy community members, some of whom vouched for him when Barker was under suspicion for minor crimes. Two who spoke most highly of him were respected business leaders whose support of a suspect would help convince an investigator that he might be wrong about the individual.

GEORGE RETURNED TO THE BUSH COMPANY that evening and bought Julia Damarell a drink.

"Did Phineas Barker have something going with Alicia Somerville?" he asked.

"He might have," Julia said. "I didn't see it but a couple of the girls said they thought Alicia might be getting together with him after her shifts ended."

George made a note in his pocket pad and asked: "Could you put a list together for me of the women who disappeared recently without telling anyone where they were going."

"Sure, if you think it would help. What did you have in mind."

"I'm going to do a little research and see if I can find out where they went."

Chapter 24

———•———

TWO DAYS LATER JULIA CALLED GEORGE at the Trooper office and gave him the names of five more young women who worked at the club during the previous two years and stopped showing up without notifying anyone of plans to quit or leave town. One of the five was Cynthia Wooden, Alicia Somerville's friend.

George knew that many of the dancers on the strip-club circuit were controlled by Vincent Denton, a Seattle mob figure who moved the women from one city to another depending on the needs of the varying club owners. He was a secretive man who did not always tell the club executives what he was doing, who he was sending them or when they might be leaving. When Denton was unhappy with them for some reason the dancers were often put on a flight to Seattle without notice.

George donned civilian clothes, flew to Seattle, rented a car and drove to a nightclub in the Ballard neighborhood. There he asked for Vincent Denton and was directed to a middle-aged man at a corner table. He introduced himself and showed his badge. Denton was noticeably unhappy to meet the Alaska State Trooper but shook his hand and invited him to take a seat.

"How can I help you, Trooper Tallent?" he asked, his tone suggesting he had little enthusiasm for the interview.

"I'm not here to give you any trouble, Mr. Denton. I think we might have a problem in Alaska, one that affects your operation there."

Denton seemed skeptical. "And what might that be?"

"At least a half dozen women have disappeared from The Bush Company in Anchorage over the last year. Their co-workers assume you just pulled them out of Anchorage or sent them to Fairbanks, Juneau or somewhere in Washington or Oregon."

"You have some names?"

George handed Denton a sheet of paper with the names and approximate ages of the women.

Denton scanned the sheet, pursed his lips and said. "I recognize a couple of them, both gals that my agency assigned to Anchorage. But we haven't heard from either one in quite a while. They just dropped out of sight. That happens sometimes in this business, often for family reasons. I don't recognize the other four offhand but wait here a minute and I'll see what I can find out."

Denton rose from the table and disappeared into a hallway at the rear of the building. Ten minutes later he returned and handed the list back to George. "My office manager tells me that we assigned all six of these women to The Bush Company but we haven't heard from any of them since they left Seattle. If they were back here they'd have called looking for new assignments. None of them have been in touch with my office."

"Do you have contact information on any of them?"

"Probably. I'll have my manager dig that out for you. He should have it tomorrow."

Denton wrote his office manager's name and phone number on a table napkin and handed it to Tallent, who rose and headed for the door. It had been a long trip for a small amount of information, but George was certain that Denton would not have been forthcoming in his answers unless the request was made face-to-face. He took a room for the night at The Hotel Seattle and called the number in the morning. Denton's office manager read him

a list of phone numbers for the six women before politely saying goodbye and hanging up the phone. All of the women were
indeed gone missing and the three-hour flight from Anchorage
had been worthwhile.

The first name on the list was Alicia Somerville, missing wife of
the Anchorage doctor; the second was a Hilda Dankman, whom
he dialed. The call was taken by Hilda's sister, Agnes. "Hello," Agnes
said tremulously, both age and worry sounding in her voice.

"This is Alaska State Trooper George Tallent. I'm trying
to locate Hilda and wondered if you had heard from her lately.
She was working in a nightclub in Anchorage, The Great Alaska
Bush Company, and her friends there are concerned that she has
dropped out of sight."

"I haven't talked to Hilda at all lately," Agnes replied, "and I'm
very worried. It has been at least a couple of months since the last
time she called. She is always pretty good about telling me where
she is and what she is up to, but I've heard nothing recently."

George scribbled several notes in his pad, thanked the woman
and hung up.

His second call was to a number in the Ballard neighborhood
of Seattle. It was answered by a gruff-sounding
man.

George introduced himself again, then asked: "Are you related
to Alice Longen?"

The man hesitated, obviously worried. "She's my daughter," the
man said. "Do you have any news of her?"

"No," George replied. "She seems to have gone missing from
her job in Anchorage, as have several others she worked with. I was
hoping you might have heard from her."

"Oh, my god," the man said. "I've heard nothing from her for
nearly two months. That is very unusual for Alice. She usually calls
at least once a week. I was thinking of flying up to Anchorage to see
what I could find out."

"I would be glad to keep you informed of anything I learn about
her whereabouts," George said. "If you do fly to Anchorage I'd be
glad to help in any way I can."

"It might be better if I stay here in Ballard," the woman's father said. "She knows how to reach me here but if I'm in Anchorage I'd just miss her call. Please keep me informed of anything you learn about her whereabouts. Even bad news would be better than knowing nothing,"

The next four calls all had similar results. The missing dancers had not contacted their friends or relatives lately and all were concerned about them. George tried not to alarm the individuals but the lack of information was worrisome to all of them and being contacted by a police investigator added to their concern.

George caught a flight back to Anchorage and had dinner that evening with Lieutenant Gilmour. He filled Gilmour in on the results of his trip and the status of the investigation. The next evening he donned civilian clothes and drove to the Northern Lights Diner on the south side of Anchorage. He ordered coffee and asked the waitress: "Is Phineas Barker here tonight?"

"He's in the kitchen. You want to talk to him?"

"Yes, please."

The woman disappeared through a door at the back of the diner and moments later a man in early middle age peered through the glass portal, spotted Tallent, opened the door and walked toward the trooper's spot at the counter.

Barker wiped his hands on his white apron as he approached. "How can I help you?"

Tallent gave his name, then showed his badge and said: "I'm an Alaska State trooper and would like to ask you a few questions. You go to The Bush Company very often?"

"I go there now and then, and I think I saw you there recently. Why do you ask?"

"Have you ever met Alicia Somerville?"

The baker had a puzzled look on his face. "Not that I know of. Should I know her?"

Tallent didn't answer but looked down at his notebook. "How about Hilda Dankman?"

"I don't know," Barker replied. "I talk to a lot of women there and buy some of them drinks. They don't always give their names and even when they do I usually don't remember them. What's this all about."

Tallent read off the other four names and got similar answers on each. "All six of these women have disappeared and I'm trying to get a handle on what might have happened to them and where they are now."

"Afraid I can't help you," Barker said. "Now I have to get back to work. I'm in the middle of something."

Tallent pocketed his notebook and headed for the door. Barker had seemed sincere, if a little nervous, and owned a reputation as a sportsman and a competent small-plane pilot. Court records showed he had served time in prison. He was arrested at age 21 for setting fire to an old school building where he once attended classes and held numerous unpleasant memories. He served two years and was released on parole. While behind bars he developed a rare and valuable talent for a criminal; he learned how to tell authorities what they wanted to hear, something he knew intuitively. It worked well with both prison guards and the psychiatrists who occasionally interviewed him to determine whether he was ready to return to society.

AFTER HIS RELEASE BARKER MOVED TO MINNESOTA and settled down. He married his high-school sweetheart when she graduated from college in 1967. The two then decided on a great adventure. They loaded their belongings into his car and headed north toward the southern end of the Alaska Highway. They drove the highway's thousand miles of unpaved roadway, a jolting trip that rattled their teeth, and arrived in Anchorage weeks later.

In Alaska's largest city Barker took a job at a Safeway store in the bakery department. His wife found a teaching job in the Eastchester neighborhood and Barker joined a sportsman's group where he became active in hunting and made friends with John Carver, an accountant.

Chapter 25

THE FOLLOWING SPRING RICK DECIDED IT WAS TIME for him to learn to fly. He often spent time in wild country and it occurred to him that if he knew how to fly he could travel across much of the state. And if he could set aside the money he might even be able to buy his own plane. For the time being he would rent light aircraft but that was expensive and minimally productive. Something like a Cessna 150, a powerful light plane that could land in small spaces, would be ideal.

He signed up for classes at Anchorage's Merrill Field and took a day off from the office to get started. The classes were given with a modified Cessna which had matching controls in the front and back seats. The instructor assigned Rick to the front seat while he took the back.

Rick had been practicing on a dummy set of controls in the flight school's office and when he sat in the front of an aircraft racing down the runway, his heart beat fiercely. But the instructor lifted the plane into the air skillfully, climbed to the desired elevation and told Rick to take the controls. When Rick's hands closed on the stick and the throttle, his heart slowed, his muscles relaxed and he made adjustments as the instructor instructed him.

He couldn't believe he was actually in charge of an aircraft—and doing it well. The instructor nodded to himself and simply gave verbal commands until he decided to land. Rick yielded control somewhat disappointed, but his instructor told him he would soon be doing everything himself.

Rick was expecting fifteen hours of flight time with the instructor before he would solo but once his total reached ten hours the instructor said he was ready and could fly the Cessna 150 by himself the next day.

He was nervous when the time came but the instructor told him that was standard. The instructor said the aircraft was ready for him and that he was to circle the field for an hour and stay within twenty-five miles of it. Rick took off from Merrill Field, circled it for an hour and landed skillfully. His instructor gave him a wide smile and a hearty handshake. He also handed him a paper indicating he had successfully completed his solo flight. His life of flying the skies of Alaska was about to begin.

By then his bank account contained enough ready cash for the down payment on a second-hand Piper PA-18 Super Cub, his dream aircraft. The Cub was a single-engine plane with two in-line seats. Through the years Phineas Barker spent much of his free time hunting and fishing, flying his Super Cub to get to Alaska's back country where the fish and wildlife grew big. For an experienced pilot, which Barker soon became, the Cub was capable of landing on remote riverbanks and beaches. Southcentral Alaska had many rivers with bankings suitable for such landings; it was the ideal environment for a skilled bush pilot.

Tallent's brief encounter with Barker stuck fast in his memory and he had difficulty sleeping the first night following their meeting. There was something about the man that seemed downright creepy. In the morning Tallent vowed to learn more about Phineas Barker and his visits to The Bush Company.

Lieutenant Gilmour laughed when George told him he was returning to the strip club again the next night. "Can't get enough of the place, eh? Some pretty ladies there who leave a lot hanging out for the gentlemen to see."

Tallent smiled. "This investigation has its advantages. And that Phineas Barker guy has me wanting to find out what happened to those women."

At The Bush, as its customers liked to call it, Tallent caught Julia Damarell's attention and she took a seat beside him.

"I'm so glad you came tonight," Julia said. "I was going to call you. I had a very weird experience with that Barker guy."

"What happened?"

"The other night I left after quitting time and saw him sitting in his car in the parking lot. He spotted me and started up his car. I wasn't thinking much about it, got into my own car and headed home. I got there, undressed, put on my bathrobe and was ready to jump into the shower when I heard a knock on the door. I opened it a crack and there he was."

"He said he was looking for someone in the apartment building and asked if I had a directory for the building. The management issues them and I did have one, so I pointed to the coffee table it was sitting on."

"He flipped through it, said he couldn't find his friend's name and asked me for a date. I told him 'No' and he left."

"Then last night when I got home he was waiting outside my place. When I started to ask him 'what's up' he pulled out a gun and stuck it in my face. He said: 'Shut up or I'll blow your brains out.'"

"He was trying to drag me into his car when my neighbor looked out the window and yelled 'Julia, what's up? Do you need help?'"

"Before I could answer her, Barker let me go, got into his car and took off."

Tallent scribbled a note and asked: "Did he hurt you?"

"No," she replied, "but he scared the crap out of me."

"Why didn't you call the police?" Tallent asked.

"I thought about it," Julia said, "but people in my line of work try to stay away from the cops. I figured I would just tell you when I saw you."

"I could bring him in," Tallent said. "I'd have to press some kind of charge against him, maybe assault and battery and threatening. But then you would have to testify in court."

"I'd rather not do that if you don't mind."

"OK," Tallent responded, "but write down everything you just told me and hang onto it just in case we need the information later on. I'll have it in my notes as well, but I'd like for you to have it down as a memory refresher."

"I will," Julia replied. "That guy is crazy. I hope you do nail the bastard."

Chapter 26

————◆————

TALLENT WAS FRUSTRATED BY THE LACK of real progress on the missing-strippers investigation and needed a break from work. So he checked out the State Troopers' SuperCub for what he described to the hangar chief as a surveillance mission, then took off from Merrill Field and headed out over Cook Inlet.

He initially flew south along the coast of the Kenai Peninsula and simply enjoyed the beauty of the coastline, the green forests and the multicolored mountains in the distance. As he approached the resort community of Homer he turned right and headed north along the Inlet's western shore.

The views along the west shore were equally spectacular until he got far enough north to get a good look at Mount McKinley in the distance. Denali, the Alaska Native name for the mountain, is more than 20,000 feet high and the highest mountain in North America. It can be seen even from many spots in Anchorage but from the air on a sunny day its white mass and surrounding glaciers are an impressive sight.

Tallent was still focusing on McKinley when he crossed over the Susitna River and decided it was time to check out the terrain ahead and below. A few minutes later he flew over Beaver Lake and spotted a plane on the lake's sandy beach. From the air the aircraft below looked a lot like Phineas Barker's SuperCub. The location of the aircraft seemed odd since there was no obvious reason for it to land on the beach except for fishing, which seemed unlikely. Tallent lowered his altitude to swing over the plane. The aircraft looked undamaged and unremarkable but in the wooded area nearby he spotted a man. As Tallent's plane neared, the man seemed to duck behind a tree to avoid being seen. That aroused his suspicions so he made a steep turn, landed on the lake's beach and taxied up to the parked plane.

The man walked out of the woods as Tallent opened his aircraft's door and started to climb out. He seemed to be wearing city clothing, which was unusual for pilots flying in wild country. When he drew closer, Tallent saw that it was indeed Phineas Barker.

"Can I help you?" Barker asked gruffly.

Tallent stepped to the ground and replied: "I saw your SuperCub parked on the beach and you moving around in the woods and just thought I'd stop and see if everything was alright."

"No problems here, officer. I just made a practice landing on the beach and thought I would step in the woods to take a leak."

Tallent looked the man over and could see nothing to make him suspicious. "Mind if I look at your ID?"

The man hesitated, then reached into his pocket, pulled out his wallet and flashed his automobile driver's license. "I have a pilot's license in here if you want to see it."

"No thanks. This will do." Tallent read the license and made a mental note of Barker's home address and the tail number of his airplane.

Barker stuffed the wallet in his pocket and Tallent said: "If you don't need any help, I guess I'll be heading back to town."

Tallent stared at the man for several seconds before heading back to his own aircraft, prompting Barker to say "What??" His voice sounded annoyed.

"Nothing" Tallent replied as he walked back to the SuperCub. He climbed in, wrote down Barker's information, then cranked the engine and let it run for several minutes before turning and taxiing back to a point where he could turn into the wind and make his takeoff.

Tallent glanced once more at Barker before pushing the throttle level to full-forward. His aircraft raced down the beach and launched into the air over the green waters of Cook Inlet.

It was nearing dark when George landed at Merrill Field and taxied to the State Troopers' hangar. He checked the plane in, reserved it for the next morning and called his office to request a coroner to accompany him the next morning on a flight across Cook Inlet.

He returned to his office where sizable pile of folders sat on a corner of his desk. The files included the paperwork related to the dancers who disappeared from The Bush Company—or perhaps left town without letting anyone know they were leaving. He had serious doubts that the women had left voluntarily.

Chapter 27

———·———

THE NEXT DAY, WHEN HE PULLED INTO THE HANGAR parking lot at 8 a.m. he waved at Dr. Vern Magnuson, who was waiting near the door.

"Morning, Doc" he said as he emerged from his vehicle. "Got your gear with you?"

The coroner waved and helped up a forensic tools bag in one hand and a shovel in the other. "These ought to do it," he replied.

Tallent smiled grimly and took the shovel from Magnuson's hand. The two men entered the hangar, opened the waiting aircraft's door, placed the shovel and bag inside, then climbed in. A mechanic near the hangar door, pulled a chain to open the door and climbed into his small tractor, which was clamped to the Cessna's front wheel. When the man turned toward the plane Tallent gave the thumb's up sign from the cockpit and the tractor fired up its engine and towed the Cessna out to the aircraft parking area off the runway. There the driver released the tow connection and headed back to the tractor parking area.

As the tow vehicle retreated, Tallent started the Cessna's engine. He let it run to warm up and shouted to the coroner. "I'm pretty sure we'll find more than one," he said.

Magnuson grimaced and responded: "We may have to get a bigger aircraft out there to get more people and shovels involved. Let's just scout it out first."

Tallent replied: "I have a crew on standby for when we need them."

As they approached Beaver Lake, Tallent reduced the Cessna's altitude and flew over the beach where he had seen Phineas Barker and his aircraft. He wanted to make sure the man had left no surprises on the beach.

Seeing none from the air he made a tight circle and landed, taking the precaution of landing as close as he could get to the tracks made by his aircraft and Barker's the previous day. He taxied near the spot where he had seen Barker in the woods and stopped his engine.

"This is the place," he told Magnuson. The two dropped their tools to the ground and climbed out. "Follow me," he said.

Just inside the trees and about twenty feet from where he had first seen Barker, Tallent spotted an area of freshly turned tundra. He hoisted the shovel, put his foot to one side and pulled out a large chunk of wet earth, spruce needles and wild grass. With each shovel-full he increased his pace.

Within minutes his digging encountered what looked like human flesh. Additional digging proved it to be the body of a woman, apparently a young one. The coroner tapped Tallent on the shoulder and the young Trooper stepped aside, handing him the shovel. Magnuson used it to clear the area around the corpse, then used his gloved hands to pull the body from the ground.

The coroner turned to Tallent and said: "I'd like to use my tools on the remains to see what I can determine, then I want to take a bunch of photographs before we package it up and load it into the plane. You might want to walk up and down the forested area beside this beach to see if there are any others."

"Mind if I take the shovel?"

"No, go ahead. My tools will be fine for me."

A half hour later, Tallent returned looking both sad and angry. "I found two more recently dug spots," he said. "I dug part-way and could see—and smell—human flesh. Those two are also graves and there are probably more. I'm going to radio the AST office. They have a crew on standby at Lake Hood and I'd like them to launch and get over here."

About twenty minutes later a De Havilland Beaver on floats landed in the lake and taxied to the beach where their Cessna was parked. Two men got out, approached Tallent for instructions and followed him to the suspected gravesites he had already found. One man began digging up those and the other went in search of similar, if older, resting places of murdered women.

By the end of the day they had found two more and the coroner confirmed that all five graves contained young women who had been cruelly murdered and buried at the edge of Alaska's wild country.

Tallent very much wanted to see the inside of Phineas Barker's house on the south side of Anchorage. He went to the courthouse the next morning and met with a judge in his office. The judge issued a search warrant.

Tallent went to the house with a locksmith and found nobody home and the door locked. With the no-knock warrant in his breast pocket, he asked his technician to pick the lock. The man finished his work quickly and Tallent asked him to wait while he entered the house.

The previous fall, Tallent had attended an FBI seminar on behavioral science and criminals. The instructor had told the assembled police officers that serial killers often take souvenirs from their victims, items that can be hidden and looked at occasionally to relive their experiences. Such items might include jewelry, clothing items or even driver's licenses.

Tallent started his search in the living room and proceeded through the entire first floor, opening doors and closets as he went, looking behind radiators, into drawers and in any crevices or openings where small items could be stored.

He found nothing of police interest until he encountered a folding ladder hanging from a ceiling on the second floor. When he pulled the ladder down, a trapdoor opened in the ceiling. Tallent climbed into what he found to be an unfinished attic, a sizable space with the open spaces between rafters filled with bulk insulation.

Though the attic was uncomfortably hot and the insulation sticky and irritating to his skin, he carefully worked his way across the floor, reaching behind each section of insulation and feeling for anything that might serve as a murder souvenir. He found nothing until he reached a small space near the far wall. When his hands made their way beneath the insulation he felt something that made his eyes go wide. He pulled out a small black bag containing several earrings and a necklace. And the bag was sitting atop an aviation map of Southcentral Alaska. Tallent unfolded the map and found it had small X marks in eight widely spaced places. Five were near the beach where they had already found women's bodies. The other three were at widely separated spots around Cook Inlet.

Chapter 28

———•———

T ALLENT SLEPT LITTLE THAT NIGHT and headed for the helipad at Trooper Headquarters before 8 a.m. The helicopter
pilot was waiting and had already completed his preflight checks
on the aircraft.

"Where to?" the pilot asked.

Tallent unfolded the map from Phineas Barker's attic and
pointed to the closest X-mark on the map. It was a gravel bar in
the middle of the Susitna River across Cook Inlet from Anchorage.
The pilot gave the thumbs-up signal, revved up the copter's engine
and lifted off.

The river's mouth is southwest of the city and is a wide opening
at the end of the 300-mile water course. They flew over the mouth
and headed north, following the map to the gravel island marked
with Barker's X. Its surface had been scraped clean by high water
and winter ice, leaving no sign of an excavation. Tallent pulled a
small shovel from the helicopter's storage compartment, looked
around and began digging holes.

The first two showed no results so Tallent thought to himself
how a murderer might select a place to bury a body. The man's
choices would be limited to the north and south ends of the gravel

bar since maneuvering the SuperCub or dragging the body to the center would then be unnecessary. Which end the plane stopped at would depend on which direction the wind was blowing. The prevailing wind in that area was from the northwest and the Cub would want to land into the wind so the grave location seemed likely to be on the northern end of the gravel landing site.

Tallent dug three more holes before his shovel made a small opening in a pile of decomposed flesh with grayish white bones exposed in places. At the highest level of the grave he found an empty .338 cartridge, presumably left there on purpose. The pilot joined him and the two removed samples from the site, slid them into a body bag and marked the location. Tallent slipped the expended cartridge into a Ziploc bag and stuffed it into a pocket in his jacket.

A crew with special expertise would return to the gravel bar and complete the exhumation. Tallent wanted to take only enough material to send to the laboratory for preliminary examination.

The two men climbed back into the helicopter and flew to the next-closest X-mark, a gravel bar on the west side of the Susitna River five miles north of the first grave site. After examining the landing site, Tallent went to the north edge and began digging again. Within minutes he found the decomposing remains of another woman. He grimaced, confident that this was indeed another of the missing dancers.

The pilot and his determined passenger spent the balance of that day and several hours the next morning landing at spots marked on Barker's map. Each one yielded human remains which would be sent to the state lab, examined and tested for DNA, which could be matched against samples on clothing or other personal items left behind by the missing dancers.

When the lab reports came back, each of the eight grave sites was determined to contain the remains of a missing Bush Company dancer. It was time for Trooper Tallent to talk to Phineas Barker. He drove to the house once again, a city police cruiser following close behind. With two uniformed officers standing beside him, Tallent rapped on Barker's door, then rang the doorbell. Moments later the door opened narrowly and a voice asked: "What do you want?"

Tallent pushed the door open, walked through it and said in a commanding voice: "Mr. Barker, you are under arrest for the kidnapping, rape and murder of eight women. Their names are on the list that I'm handing you. Please turn around and put your hands behind you."

Barker complied, then spent the night in a holding cell and appeared in a courtroom next day. Tallent and a lawyer from the state attorney general's office spelled out the evidence against Barker and the judge ordered him held for further investigation and possible trial.

When the accused murderer appeared in court the following spring, the prosecutor presented the mass of evidence uncovered by Tallent and a jury ultimately found Barker guilty on all charges. The judge sentenced him to prison without possibility of parole and Barker began the final chapter of his life as a prisoner at the Spring Creek Correctional Center in Seward, Alaska. He would eventually die there.

Chapter 29

———•———

IN MID-JANUARY, TALLENT TOOK AN ALASKA AIRLINES FLIGHT to Juneau for a series of meetings with leaders of the Alaska State Troopers. The state Legislature was then in session and the few hotels were filled with legislators and the lobbyists who attached themselves to the politicians.

"Juneau is a busy place at this time of year," he commented in one meeting with high-level department personnel.

"Oh yeah," said one officer in civilian clothes. "And everybody wants something. Not with us," he said, "but the politicians are very popular."

"Anything special going on?" Tallent asked.

"That oil discovery in Cook Inlet has got this place buzzing," the man said. "It's a pretty big deal. I understand they've found billions of barrels of oil in the earth under the water. Biggest find ever in Alaska. Could have a tremendous impact on state budgets."

"Including money for law enforcement?"

"From what I hear," the man replied, "it will be boosting budgets across the board. And that includes law enforcement. Our commissioner will make sure of that."

"Wow," Tallent said. "He should find a seat near Governor Gruening and keep whispering in his ear to make it happen."

"There will be a lot of competition for the big bucks," the man said. "People are becoming lobbyists who have never been near the Legislature. If they know anybody in state government they have a leg up. Actually law enforcement could play a major role in what happens here. A team of lobbyists are working to get a Republican elected to take Bill Egan's job in the governor's office."

"You're kidding," Tallent whispered. "This was a Democratic territory and the Democrats have controlled the governor's office since statehood. Getting a Republican into that job would take some doing."

"Well this place is filling up with doers," the man said. Anything could happen."

"Hang onto your idea about Wally Hickel, the hotel guy in Anchorage," Tallent told him. "He apparently is interested in the top job and if any Republican could move to the top in Alaska it would be Wally. He has his friends down here stirring the pot in his direction. Lots of Republican money around if he decided to jump in."

"What about Bill Egan?" the man asked.

"The Democrats are all behind Egan," Tallent said. "Bill is a good man but so is Wally. If the two of them ever went head-to-head there would be political blood all over and I'm not sure how it would come out. It would be an interesting campaign, that's for sure."

"There are a lot of Democrats who are worried about the growing power of the oil industry in Alaska politics," the man countered. "Hickel is an oil guy at heart. I understand he has money invested in it. No question which side he would be on."

"Well, oil could bring a lot of jobs," Tallent replied. "And a ton of new state revenues. All of those oilfields under the Inlet are state leases. So the state treasury is going to get fat both from lease revenues and taxes. The Legislature won't be able to spend money fast enough to get ahead of what's rolling in."

"Wow," the man said. "A great time to be in Alaska."

"If you like to see politics in action and a booming economy," Tallent laughed. "All in all a good thing."

"Are you going to stay in law enforcement?" the man asked. "There should be a lot of high-paying jobs coming available."

"Not my thing," Tallent said. "I like what I do."

"There will be a lot of oil money moving around in Juneau," the man predicted. "You can bet on that."

"I'm sure that will be the case," Tallent noted, a grim smile on his face. "Hope it doesn't get out of hand."

"Good luck with that," the man said.

Chapter 30

IN OCTOBER, RICK ALBERT, GEORGE TALLENT and Hank Rosenthal caught a series of flights to the remote village of Kiana on the Kobuk River in Northern Alaska. Their reservations were at a hunting lodge owned by a friend of George's on the west bank of the Kobuk, a popular spot for hunting both moose and caribou. They arrived in mid-day and shook hands with the lodge owner, Lorry Anderson, a jovial Alaskan Eskimo with a magnetic personality.

Rick and his friends were planning to go in search of moose or caribou early the next morning. After a few short hikes to familiarize themselves with the area and its terrain they returned to the lodge. On the way into the building they passed a guest who was standing on the deck with host Lorry, waving binoculars and pointing to a four-legged figure with antlers near the riverbank below them. It was a bull moose, a large one.

Rick, George and Hank were not ready to hunt and the distance between the lodge and the riverbank was large and open. If they tried to sneak up on the big animal it would surely see them and be spooked. It seemed just an invitation to a lot of fruitless work. The man with the binoculars pulled a moose call from his pocket and began making noises that sounded more like a sheep's bleat to the three men from Anchorage. The noise is supposed to sound like a female moose in heat, one that will attract an ardent male.

The three men were seated in an alcove off the dining room drinking bourbon when the guest with the binoculars and moose call wandered in and joined them. He told them Lorry was out- side loading a wheelbarrow with firewood from a stack behind the lodge. The four in the alcove got along well and were sharing one of their many stories while awaiting their host's return.

After a half-hour another hunter rushed into the alcove and pointed to the fourth man. "Hey," he said, "your calling brought that moose into the back yard and he's all worked up. You better get out there and shoot him before he screws Lorry." Rick Albert and his friends laughed uproariously while the man scrambled to fetch his rifle from a rack and then slipped out the door to the deck. A few minutes later they heard a shot, followed by the fourth hunter racing back into the lodge to gather the tools he would need to butcher the dead moose.

Over the next four days all three of the Anchorage friends man- aged to harvest a moose and performed the laborious procedure for cleaning and cutting their animals into steaks and roasts. They packed the meat into coolers brought for the purpose and waited for their pilot's return.

On their return flight to Anchorage, Rosenthal mentioned in passing that his company, Humble Oil, was changing its name to Exxon.

"What's that all about?" Rick asked. The change was a surprise since Humble Oil had long been a name known throughout Alaska. The company had played a major role in the state's economy, which had thrived with the oil discoveries.

"I'm not supposed to know this," Rosenthal said, "so if I tell you two guys you both have to swear you'll never tell anyone."

Rick and George both nodded and said they would keep the secret.

"Humble is one of the world's largest companies," Hank said, "and that name in the english language suggests humility, which a lot of people thought was inappropriate. So they ran a bunch of possibilities through a computer and Exxon sounds like a real name but doesn't mean anything in any language. So Exxon it is and will be."

All three men enjoyed a laugh and settled in for the flight back to Anchorage. Rick opened a wall panel that concealed a bar and poured each of them a drink.

Chapter 31

———•———

RICK'S EXPERIENCE IN THE SCHOOL DISTRICT JOB and his family's military background encouraged him to apply for the position of superintendent of schools at Fort Richardson, an army base on the north flank of the city. He applied and won the job. His position in the education system encouraged Rick to teach a course in political science, which he did for several years, and when a seat came open in the Alaska Senate, he decided to go into politics and run for the job. The effort was successful and the one-time president of the senior class at Anchorage High School became a state senator and launched himself on what was to become a very successful political career.

One morning in February of 1967 Tallent went to his office and found a note on his desk asking him to call Peter Arthur, president of the Valdez State Bank. The call had originated in an Anchorage banker's office whom George knew well.

He called the Valdez number and said: Mr. Arthur, I'm George Tallent of Alaska State Troopers. I had a note that you called."

In Valdez the man looked around to see if any of his colleagues were watching or listening, then replied: "Yes, Trooper Tallent. I called your headquarters in Juneau about a problem our auditors have encountered. We can't find or account for $48,000. I think the situation calls for an investigation by somebody with your credentials."

"I'll be on the next flight to Valdez," George said, "and will call later today to let you know when I can get to your office. It will probably be first thing tomorrow morning. Since banking is not my specialty I will probably have one or two experts with me."

"Thank you. I would appreciate the help. Forty-eight thousand is a lot of money for us to be missing."

Tallent had met the bank president once at a state business conference but had never really talked with the man. He called the department's travel office and requested a round-trip ticket to Valdez. He also called his supervisor and asked for assistance with experts in banking matters.

"We have access to two forensic investigators," the supervisor said. "I'll see if they are available and can come to Valdez with you on the next flight."

The supervisor called back fifteen minutes later. "Both of the auditors are available and could join you on that two p.m. flight to Valdez."

"Great," Tallent said. "I'll tell the bank president we can be at his office by four."

GEORGE AND THE TWO FORENSICS EXPERTS met at the Alaska Airlines ticket office shortly before boarding time. They introduced themselves, caught the flight and arrived in the mountain-rimmed town of Valdez less than an hour later.

In Valdez they checked out a rental car and drove to the bank office. There on the building's second floor Tallent introduced himself and the two auditors to the secretary outside the president's office. She spoke into an intercom and a grim-faced man with gray hair appeared at the office door.

"Please come in," the banker said. "I'm Alfred Tucker, president of this institution. Thank you for responding so promptly."

"Mr. Tucker, I'm George Tallent of Alaska State Troopers and these two gentlemen are forensics investigators who handle a lot of our high-tech work, Mr. Callihan and Mr. Morgan."

George and the two forensics men followed President Tucker into his office and took a seat opposite an imposing desk.

"Any indication where the missing money might have gone?" Tallent asked.

"I wish we knew" Tucker said. "Our accountants have gone over our records and the forty-eight thousand just appears to be missing with no tracks left. We have no idea where it went."

The bank president led the three men into a large conference room where a team of accountants had paperwork spread over the desktop. Together they worked until early evening assessing the problem.

The State Trooper team stayed the night at the Valdez Inn and returned in the morning to resume their efforts. George stayed with the forensics experts until after lunch working to get a full understanding of the problem. There seemed to be no explanation other than the money simply disappeared, presumably stolen.

After lunch he excused himself and said: "I think I'll wander around town and talk to a few people. That would be a better use of my time while you numbers people see if you can come up with a few clues for me."

Tallent left the bank wearing his full uniform and took a leisurely stroll through the town. He entered a coffee shop and introduced himself to the manager.

"Welcome to Valdez, Trooper Tallent," the manager said. "What brings you to our neck of the woods?"

"Just doing a project at the bank. Thought I'd get out and stretch my legs, meet a few people. It's been a long time since I spent any time here."

"Hope nothing is wrong at the bank," the man said. "My life savings are in there."

"We're working on a few issues. Hopefully we'll get them all resolved."

"Anything I can do to help?"

"Perhaps there is. Are you aware of any big-money transactions taking place in town."

"None that I think of," the manager replied. "Nothing except the big poker game at Vinny Horgan's place every Saturday. Those guys spread some large cash around at times."

"Who is Vinny Horgan?"

"He owns a tavern over on Black Spruce Avenue. An upscale place with a sizable back room and a large poker table. He and his buddies put lots of money on the table sometimes. I've never played with them but I've heard from some who do. It's called The Spruce Tavern. They serve good food and the booze ain't bad either. They serve a lot of it."

"Thank you. I think I'll run by there."

Tallent walked the three blocks to The Spruce Tavern, entered the relatively new building and asked a bartender for the manager.

"That would be Vinny. He's sitting over there in a booth."

Tallent strode to the booth, introduced himself to the manager and took a seat opposite him.

"What can I do for you, Man in Blue?" Horgan asked.

"I'm here with a team working in the bank. I just thought I'd wander around and see what I could learn. My primary interest at the moment is in any large cash transactions. I understand your Saturday night poker games sometimes involve sizable pots of cash."

"They do indeed," Horgan said. "Any specific information you'd like?"

"Yes, for one thing I wondered who the regular players are."

"Well, there's me. Then there is Buddy Gustavus from the Visitors Bureau; Chuck Eddy, who is retired; Nat Walker, the insurance guy; Charlie Tucker from the bank and Nate Edrington. Nate owns a small restaurant on the south side of town."

"Is Charlie Tucker any relation to Alfred Tucker, president of the bank."

"His son. About forty years old, I think."

Tallent blinked in surprise. "Has Charlie Tucker had any big losses at the poker table in recent months?"

"Oh, yeah," Horgan replied. "Charlie has had kind of a run of bad luck. Worked pretty well for a couple of us who have been winning but it has been pretty rough on Charlie."

"Does Charlie Tucker do any gambling besides your Saturday night poker games?"

"Some," Horgan said. "He made a trip to Las Vegas recently."

"How did he do?"

"I'm not sure. He didn't say much about the trip but he was in a terrible mood when he got back. His temper was flaring during our game last Saturday."

Tallent returned to the bank and asked Alfred Tucker to introduce him to his son.

"Why certainly," Tucker said. "Please follow me."

THE BANK PRESIDENT LED TALLENT TO AN OFFICE near the rear of the building, introduced him to his son Charles and withdrew. The younger Tucker knew instinctively what the State Trooper wanted to talk to him about and sat nervously waiting.

"How can I help you?" he asked.

"I understand you play a lot of high-stakes poker and have lost quite a bit of money lately," Tallent said. "I also understand you dropped a bundle at a casino in Vegas a few weeks ago. I talked to the casino manager and he told me you lost something like fifty thousand dollars while you were there. That's a lot of money for a guy who lives on a salary."

Tallent was lying about talking to the casino manager but young Tucker believed him. He started to choke, then tears flowed from his eyes.

"I intended to pay it back," he squealed. "I would never steal anything. I was just borrowing the money but it got out of control—and I kept losing. Can I talk to my dad? I want to explain."

Tallent nodded agreement. "I have a few questions to ask and then you can talk to your father."

George asked a series of pointed questions whose answers gave details on how the thefts were carried out and covered up. At their conclusion he extracted a signed confession, took Charlie Tucker to his father's office and waited outside while the young banker explained his embezzlement to his horrified father.

Afterward the elder banker approached Tallent and the forensics experts in the lobby. "What happens now?" he asked.

Tallent grimaced. "Well, if you cooperate in the prosecution, we will press charges against him. He may have to serve some time in prison."

Tears were now in the banker's eyes as well. "I can't prosecute my own son. I just couldn't do it. I won't"

The man's reaction was hugely frustrating to the seasoned Trooper but if he refused to participate in the prosecution proceedings there was no case to be made. Tallent and his investigators loaded up their briefcases and caught the next flight to Anchorage. The young banker went free, the father used his own savings to repay his son' embezzlements and the crime was never made public.

Chapter 32

IN 1968 GEORGE TALLENT WAS FOUR YEARS into his career as an Alaska State Trooper when he was assigned to a task force investigating drug dealing in the Anchorage area. The dealers were beginning to reach out to the villages and the drug problem threatened to become an epidemic. The leader of the task force, Major Chet Barnett, invited George to appear with him before a legislative committee seeking information about the extent of the drug problem. When they entered and found seats in the brightly-lighted hearing room, George was surprised to see his old friend Rick Albert seated near the center of the massive head table facing the audience.

When the chairman gaveled the meeting to order, Rick raised a hand. "Point of order?" Mr. Chairman, "or I should say point of personal privilege."

"Go ahead, Senator Albert."

Rick smiled and turned to face the two Troopers. "I just wanted to welcome these two gentlemen to this hearing. Major Barnett is one of Alaska's top police officers. With him is Trooper George Tallent. Trooper Tallent and I are old friends and were classmates throughout our high school careers. I'm pleased to see both of these men here and feel our constituents can take a degree of comfort in the fact that they are fighting the good fight against the drug dealers who appear to be invading Alaska."

The chairman nodded and replied: "I agree with Senator Albert's comments and add my personal welcome to his. I'm hoping the problem we are here to address, the growing drug plague in Alaska, will be thoroughly and professionally investigated and criminal activities of this kind can be wiped out. Major Barnett, Officer Tallent, please be seated."

"Trooper Tallent," George corrected him.

"Forgive me, sir. Make that Trooper Tallent. You are both most welcome."

The hearing was inconclusive but in the following months the State Trooper Task Force made numerous arrests resulting in convictions and lengthy prison terms for many of the drug dealers and their helpers. The problem was an insidious one involving dealers in both oil worker camps and nearby villages. It would never be eliminated entirely, but the investigation resulted in at least a temporary reduction in drug deals across much of Alaska.

George Tallent and his task force were frustrated that one of the key people in the drug ring was a Seattle mobster known as Max who had been in Alaska for the last year. The man was working with Alaska's leading criminals to set up wholesale buys from his colleagues in Seattle, many of them leaders of criminal groups spanning the entire Pacific Northwest.

"The guy knows what he is doing," the Valdez mayor told George. "He is a born public relations man and knows how to deal with both elected officials and city employees. He gets involved in community activities, puts up money to support athletic teams and charitable organizations. He has paid for plane tickets to get team members to statewide competitions in Anchorage, Nome and Juneau. He and his backers have bought buildings and land that they use primarily to store drugs and alcohol, but they also make space available for community uses and storage of athletic equipment. He is a very popular guy."

Tallent found that those who were unaware of the man's criminal activities had the impression he was a civic-minded man who shared his earnings and capabilities with the community in which he lived and made his living.

George went to Major Barnett with an idea. Max Cavendish was keeping a low profile, at least with his criminal activities, and demanded that all his contacts respect the need for secrecy about his Seattle mob ties. But George had contacts among the drug dealers, a few that he allowed to operate as long as they were willing to provide information about others. Since the other men were their competitors, the few key dealers willingly agreed—and since George was an Alaska Native and one of the few police officers they trusted—the men fed him information on a regular basis, information that led to many arrests.

Barnett thought about Tallent's idea for two days before giving his approval. George called Howard Botell, a reporter at the Anchorage Daily Nugget, and set up a meeting in a downtown coffee shop. When Botell arrived he spotted the handsome young Trooper in civilian clothes in a booth near the back wall. "What's up?" he asked.

George swept the room with his eyes and then confided: "There is a guy in Valdez you might find interesting. He is a mobbed-up hood from Washington state who is working with our local drug dealers. His connections in Seattle are linked to the drug network throughout the Pacific Northwest—and they are channeling tons of nasty stuff to the low-lifes in this area. He is wholesaling drugs to the local dealers.

Botell's face had a surprised look. "Are the Valdez locals getting too looped or something? Why focus there?"

"They were a problem," Tallent said, " but we've shut down most of the dealers in the city itself. The problem now is in a few villages and those camps established to house workers building the pipeline to carry oil from the North Slope. There are dozens of the camps along the whole 800 miles of the pipeline route and the drugs are becoming a real problem. The pipeline operators are ready to run off the local people they've already hired and brought in contract help from their headquarters in Dallas, Texas. The drugs are a bad enough deal but there are a lot of Alaskans on the construction crews and those jobs are important to our people. We need to have the problem go away without getting our locals fired."

"What's the guys name?"

"Max Cavendish. He has an apartment at the Valdez Golden Inn."

Botell scribbled a few notes, lowered his head, glanced around and asked: "Can you give me some information about his operations? I'd need a lot of details."

"You can have everything we've got," George said, trying to conceal his enthusiasm.

Trooper Tallent went to the newspaper office next day with a large briefcase. He spent several hours with the reporter, verbally feeding him details while spreading a raft of official police documents across Botell's desk. When he finished the presentation he gathered up the paperwork and leaned forward as if to rise from the chair.

"Can I keep copies of those?" Botell asked.

"I'm afraid I can't do that," he said. These are official State Trooper documents and outside of our office only a judge is supposed to see them right now. You have a lot of notes and I'll be glad to answer any questions you have. Just give me a call anytime. Here, I'll give you my home number." He scribbled it on a business card and handed it to the reporter.

Botell called that evening and Tallent spent an hour on the phone with him. Eventually the reporter suggested they call it a day and talk again in the morning. Botell called him the next day just as Tallent was heading to his office but he considered the call important business and spent another hour answering his questions. Many were simply clarifiers on items they had discussed earlier.

Chapter 33

T HE FOLLOWING SUNDAY HOWARD BOTELL'S FIRST STORY was bannered across the top of the Anchorage Daily Nugget's front page. The headline screamed: "Seattle mob invades Alaska." The series continued for four days, with extensive detail about Max Cavendish and his drug distributorship extending from one end of the pipeline construction project to the other, from the North Slope to Valdez on the Gulf of Alaska. The Seattle mobster found his telephone ringing constantly, one reporter after another asking questions based on the Botell story, none of which he answered. Cavendish caught a southbound flight on Wednesday and would never return to Alaska. More importantly, he was not replaced and the drug problem in both the villages and the pipeline camps diminished greatly.

When Tallent reported for work on Friday Major Barnett flashed him the thumbs up signal. Cavendish's sudden departure was by then well known throughout the community leadership.

Later in 1968 Rick Albert broadened his horizons and ran for Alaska's only seat in the U.S. House but was defeated by the incumbent, the Republican Howard Pollock. Two years later Congressman Pollock decided to call it a career and did not run for re-election. Rick ran for the seat against Frank Murkowski, a Republican banker who was determined to leave banking behind and serve in public office. Rick's higher political profile gave him an advantage and Rick won, forcing Murkowski to postpone his plans for public office. Murkowski would later win a Senate seat and in 2002 was elected governor of Alaska.

Rick assumed office in 1970 as the freshman congressman from Alaska. He took to the job with enthusiasm and pursued his many goals relentlessly, winning admiration from the House leadership. He was a lifelong Democrat and the party decided it would be very much in the party's interest to keep Rick Albert in Congress if it could. With his talents he would be a natural fit for the U.S. Senate and could look forward to moving to that respected chamber someday.

When the House recessed the following March, Rick flew home to Alaska and stopped in Juneau to meet with the governor.

"Welcome home, Mr. Congressman," Governor Egan said. "And thank you for stopping by."

Albert smiled broadly. "Good to see you again, Bill. I just thought I would drop in and see if you had any new priorities that I needed to know about."

"Nothing new," Rick replied. "The only real priority for action by Congress is getting that oil pipeline approved, but you already know all about that. And, believe me, if there were I wouldn't hesitate to get you on the phone."

"I know that, Governor, and I very much appreciate your attitude. My staff has standard instructions to let me know whenever you call even if I am in a meeting. Congress has Alaska's economic future in its hands and we can't take any chance that the decision will go the wrong way."

"Rick, your support for that project is very much appreciated," Egan said. "All I can say is hang in there and please call me if I can do anything to help or if there is any change in support for our position."

"You can count on that," Albert replied.

Chapter 34

———◆———

NOT LONG AFTER HE ARRIVED IN WASHINGTON, Rick started looking into opportunities to use his position for personal gain. And since some lobbyists are quick to determine which new members of Congress are looking, opportunities often come to those who want them. Rick began having lunch with every lobbyist who invited him. Nothing happened at the luncheons except development of relationships that could later be useful.

Young Rick Albert's developing ties with lobbyists, including several with industry representatives having questionable reputations, came to the attention of Ron Pitlow, senior member of the House in the Seattle delegation. One afternoon Pitlow showed up in Rick's office door.

"Can I come in?" he asked.

"Congressman Pitlow, please do come in by all means. Can I offer you a drink? I have a bottle of bourbon in this drawer." He gestured to a middle drawer in his desk.

"No, and please call me Ron," Pitlow said. "We are peers now."

"Yes, Ron, thank you. And to what do I owe the pleasure of your company today."

"Rick, I've noticed—and so have several other members of my delegation—that you seem to be getting close to an awful lot of lobbyists, including a few sleaze-bags. All members of Congress deal with lobbyists on a regular basis. The lobbyists do make campaign contributions, and those are at best a necessary evil that you have to be careful of, but their greatest value to you can be in providing vital information on the industries they represent.

Rick was shocked by his colleague's words and a bit angry. "What would you suggest?" he asked.

Pitlow grimaced. "You might want to limit your interactions with lobbyists, at least tone down your obvious enthusiasm. I would instead increase the time you give to constituent issues. Do some research and contact the leaders in Alaska communities that you met during the campaign. Ask them which federal issues they are concerned about and what the people they represent would like to see happen."

"I know that is certainly already on your mind, but what is needed is to give it a much greater priority. Devote more of your time and energy to the issues important to Alaskans."

Rick was infuriated by Congressman Pitlow's words but he decided to pretend that the man was right. "I'm sorry to hear that my efforts here have been interpreted in that light. I am working hard to deal with the issues my constituents, the people of Alaska, consider most important. The lobbyists can help with many of them and I have been recruiting their support toward that end. Perhaps I should take a different approach and spend more time working with my colleagues and the staff people available to me."

Pitlow nodded his agreement. "Thank you for considering my suggestions. I hope you don't mind my words today but I wanted to warn you that you are being perceived as headed in the wrong direction. Perhaps you are not, but perceptions are very important in our line of work."

"I agree and thank you for coming by," Rick said, burying his anger and putting a shy smile on his face.

After Ron Pitlow's visit, Rick didn't change his ways very much but he did become more discreet in his behavior, especially with

the many lobbyists who flocked to Washington during the congressional session. His relationships with them were just as strong
and potentially compromising, but when they visited his office
or met with him in restaurants he made an effort to look inquisitive and serious about his work. He was interested in exploiting
the many representatives of the oil industry and other corporate
entities but he learned to adopt facial expressions that gave him a
somewhat studious look.

Rick also learned that there was money to be made as a member of Congress in addition to his government salary. Several
of the lobbyists he developed relationships with often gave him
investment tips, information that was based on insider knowledge. Many of the lobbyists were ineligible to use their insider
knowledge for their personal investments, but when they passed
it on to friends like Rick their friends could make decisions that
swelled their bank accounts and increased their positive attitudes
toward him.

Rick was re-elected near the end of his first term and he decided
on that second election day that he wanted eventually to move up
to the United States Senate. His bank account was already large
enough to cover a run for the Senate but once he started mention-
ing his long-term intention to move up offers of campaign contributions began to flow in.

RICK ALBERT AND GEORGE TALLENT REMAINED FRIENDS
throughout Rick's political career though they spent little time
together except for traditional visits during the Christmas holi-
days. Rick's political commitments and George's police job limited opportunities for anything else. But they were always glad to
see each other and celebrated enthusiastically when holiday-time
arrived each year.

In 1966 Rick ran for Alaska's single seat in the United States
House of Representatives but was defeated by his fellow state senator, Howard Pollock, a Republican. Rick was discouraged by his
loss to Pollock but remained determined to move to Washington
as a member of the United States Congress.

Rick was shaken by his defeat at the polls and decided not to challenge Pollock when Pollock ran for re-election in 1968. Then in 1970 Pollock decided not to run for his House seat again and instead threw his hat into the race for the Republican nomination for governor. Rick Albert ran for the open seat in the U.S. House and was elected on November 3, 1970, defeating banker Frank Murkowski, who remained determined to remain in politics and would later become Alaska's governor. Pollock lost his bid for the state's governorship and did not run for office again. He remained one of the state's un-elected political leaders for the rest of his life.

Chapter 35

—◦—

RICK WAS SWORN IN TO HIS NEW CONGRESSIONAL SEAT on January 3, took possession of his new office and almost immediately received a telephone call from Governor William Egan.

"Good morning, Governor. How are things in Juneau?"

"Oh, so-so," Egan said. "And please call me Bill. We've known each other long enough. Please accept my congratulations."

"Well, thank you, Bill. We have indeed known each other for many years. May I ask, do you have any priority projects that I can help you with?"

"Well, yes, Rick, there is something I'd like to talk to you about. If you don't mind I'd rather not talk about it on the phone. I was hoping you might stop into Juneau sometime when you come this way."

"We take a two-week break at Easter if your project isn't too urgent."

The governor coughed. "It's important enough but I would rather be looking you in the eye when I'm talking to you. It's one of my idiosyncrasies. If you can stop by Juneau on your way home to Anchorage, that would work for me."

"I'd be glad to do that."

"Thanks Rick. I'll plan on it. Let me know when you'll be here and I'll block out some time for our discussion."

"Will do," the congressman said, obviously puzzled by the ominous tone in the governor's words.

"Great," Egan replied. "I'll look forward to it."

On a quiet August afternoon in Washington, House Majority Leader Harley Whitney stepped into Rick Albert's office on the second floor of Washington's Rayburn Office Building. "Good morning, fearless leader," Rick said, "to what do I owe the pleasure?"

"You know," Whitney replied, "I've never been to Alaska but I've always wanted to see it. I was thinking I might like to visit there sometime this fall, maybe during our next break. You will be up for re-election and I'd be glad to accompany you on some constituent meetings, maybe put in a good word for you if you thought that might help."

Rick smiled. He knew the majority leader was worried because the Congressman from Alaska did not always go along with the issues Whitney was pushing. He wanted to get Rick in his debt, a debt he could call in when needed. But the Alaskan was delighted by the offer. He was being challenged in the upcoming election by Don Young, a member of the Alaska State Senate and former tugboat captain on the Yukon River. Young was a popular man with a uniquely Alaskan lifestyle. He was a formidable challenger and having Harley Whitney along on a campaign swing through the state would help build Rick's reputation as a national-level player, a definite advantage in an Alaska election.

"I'd love to have you do that," Rick told Whitney. "I'm headed home when we break on Friday. Can you make it then?"

"That would work just fine," Whitney replied. "Ordinarily I'd head back to New Orleans for break but my wife is off in New England with her sister. That makes me a free man for a couple of weeks. I'm from the Bayou Country and have never been north of Seattle. I understand your state is very beautiful, well worth seeing even for a guy who has been over a lot of the world already. Put something together and I'll go there with you."

When the majority leader made his exit, Rick grabbed a phone and called his wife Myrlie. Then he rushed into an adjacent office, alerted his staff to the opportunity and made assignments. Finally he returned to his desk and called Governor William Egan, a fellow Democrat who was delighted to hear that Harley Whitney would be coming to Juneau.

"Can you put together some meetings for me?" Albert asked. "I'd like to show my bayou buddy the best we have to offer and introduce him to all the right people in Alaska."

"I'd be happy to do that," Egan said. "Just give me the dates when you'll be here and I'll make sure he shakes hands or has a drink with the cream of the crop. That will be a great opportunity. This state is still young and we need all the help we can get from Congress, especially people in high places—like the majority leader. I look forward to seeing you both. Where are you taking him besides Juneau?"

"Thanks, Bill. I want to get him to Anchorage, Fairbanks, maybe Sitka or Ketchikan. And while we're up north I'd like to work in a day on the North Slope. The majority leader is from oil country and I think he'd get a kick out of seeing the operations around Prudhoe Bay. Our reserves are going to make Louisiana's look like a wee-hole in the snow."

"You got it," the governor replied. "I'll get some people working on it and send you the contact names so your staff can follow up."

When their Alaska Airlines flight landed at Anchorage International Airport, Rick Albert and Harley Whitney were met by Governor Egan in a large Cadillac sedan kept by state officials for his use when the governor was in the city. Egan's driver took the party to the Hotel Captain Cook, named for Captain James Cook, the British explorer who first brought western civilization to the area. The hotel had been built seven year's earlier by former Republican Governor Walter J. Hickel and Hickel's ownership would ordinarily be a deterrent to occupancy by elected Democrats, but the Cook was by far Anchorage's best hotel, its restaurants were excellent and the accommodations were the best in the city. There was nothing else comparable.

Hickel's ownership might also have been worrisome for the Democrats since he was Alaska's second governor and won the job by defeating the incumbent, Alaska's first and current governor, Bill Egan himself. Egan regained the job when Hickel left office four years later. Despite the ticklish relationship, there was sufficient camaraderie among the political class in the small-population state that visiting Democrats gladly stayed there and often sought Hickel out to say hello during their stays.

This time Hickel was warned that the governor's vehicle was approaching and met the three Democrats when they stepped into the lobby. "Gentlemen," he said, "welcome to the Hotel Captain Cook. Delighted to have you here."

As the senior man present, Harley Whitney stepped forward, shook Hickel's hand and thanked him for the warm greeting. "Thank you, Governor. I hope you'll join us for a drink once we get settled into our rooms."

"I will indeed," Hickel replied. "Is this your first time in Alaska, Congressman?"

"It is," Whitney said. "Rick Albert has thoughtfully invited me and I'm looking forward to seeing as much of it as possible. I'm especially interested in seeing the North Slope and the site of your big discovery at Prudhoe Bay. That will be a major new source of oil for the nation if your industry can resolve the issues that are holding back development. I suspect Congress may be involved in some of the upcoming decisions."

A smile crossed Hickel's face. "Indeed it will, and I think you'll find there are good answers to all of your questions. Alaska would never allow construction of an 800-mile pipeline through some of its wildest and most beautiful country unless our great land is treated properly and the wild country and its creatures carefully protected."

"I look forward to hearing those answers," Whitney said.

Chapter 36

⸺⸱⸺

THE FOLLOWING MORNING RICK DROVE to the corporate office of The Anchorage Times and the two congressmen walked to the second-floor office of Robert B. Atwood, the legendary publisher of Alaska's largest newspaper.

When they appeared in the waiting area Atwood's secretary and executive assistant spotted them and rushed into the adjoining office. Atwood came out moments later with a broad smile on his face.

"Welcome back Rick, and you sir must be Speaker of the House Harley Whitney. Welcome to Anchorage and to my office, Mr. Congressman. We are delighted to have you here in the forty-ninth and by far the largest and northernmost of the states, the great state of Alaska."

"Thank you very much, Mr. Atwood," Whitney said, "and I am delighted to be here."

"Please come into my office and get comfortable," Atwood said. "I hope you have time to visit for a few minutes. And, please, call me Bob."

Rick Albert gestured for his colleague to precede him into Atwood's office. "We are delighted that you are in town and not off on one of your many journeys. Harley, Bob Atwood is a world traveler and has been in Washington numerous times."

Whitney smiled broadly and said: "I'm well aware of your many travels, Bob, and enjoy the opportunity to shake your hand once again. You and your newspaper are a marvelous voice for Alaska and you are to be commended both for your advocacy for Alaska statehood and for your day-to-day effort to advance the interests of your great state."

"Thank you for saying that, Harley," Atwood replied. "Evangeline and I look forward to seeing you at dinner tomorrow evening. We have invited a number of Alaska's community leaders to meet you as I'm sure Rick has told you."

"Yes," Whitney said, "Rick has put together a marvelous introduction to Alaska and its people for me. And while the three of us are alone together I was wondering if there were any issues you would like to discuss that might better be discussed under such circumstances."

"Well one thing that will undoubtedly be brought up by a great many people," Atwood answered, "is the importance of having congressional approval for construction of a pipeline from the North Slope to Southcentral Alaska. Our state's economy and the entire nation's economy very much need to get that oil moving to market. Both houses of Congress will be considering a measure to authorize construction of the pipeline. I hope you and your many friends will side with Alaska in this issue. The environmental community is doing its darnedest to block construction."

"We Alaskans love our natural environment," Atwood said "But the green community goes too far, the tree huggers. They want to shut down our economy and block development. I don't think they appreciate just how large Alaska really is and what a small imprint that pipeline will have on our wild country."

Whitney laughed. "You are right about that, my friend. When you are living in New York or Chicago there is no way to really understand the vast scope of Alaska and what you have here. I've been reading the statistics for years and seen many photographs, but until you see a sight like Mount McKinley or stand beside the Yukon River your perspective is too limited to appreciate them."

"That is for sure," Atwood said. "And I should mention that I have investments in Alaska oil. Many members of the business community have made them. It's our way of getting behind the companies that are hiring our people and building an economy for our future."

"A wise approach," Whitney replied. "Putting your money where your mouth is, as that crass old saying goes. You are encouraging the people who need it and who can do the most for Alaska. I would do the same thing if it weren't for the conflict it would present for a member of Congress."

"Don't look at me," Rick Albert countered defensively. "My wife makes all those decisions in my family."

Atwood and Whitney both chortled. "Sounds good to me," Atwood said. "I'd probably be way ahead if Evangeline made those decisions in my family. She is a very bright woman.

The three men spent a jovial half-hour together before Rick signaled Whitney that it was time to leave. Atwood was obviously enjoying the conversation and not anxious to end it but he knew Rick and Harley Whitney would have a full-schedule laid out for the balance of the day.

Chapter 37

———•———

THE TWO CONGRESSMEN TRAVELED THE STATE in a twin-engine Cessna-421 owned and piloted by Rick's old friend Don Walker, owner of a small flying service based in Anchorage. They spent two days touring Anchorage and its suburbs, meeting Albert's key political allies and attending a political rally in his honor. Whenever Albert introduced Majority Leader Whitney to his hometown crowd, the audience went wild and launched into prolonged applause. Each time Whitney smiled, thanked the emcee, gave a brief speech about then-pending national issues and a warm endorsement to his colleague Rick Albert.

In Fairbanks they went through a similar schedule, saw the sights of Alaska's fabled Interior City and spent a day on a riverboat traveling the Chena River. They stopped at several villages along the way, greeted local leadership and gave brief speeches to the assembled Alaska Natives, the indigenous people of the area.

When the riverboat made a stop at Chena Hot Springs the group was touring the heated springs for which the community was named when Rick spotted a young man waving at him. The wave could have been a simple sign of welcome but Congressman Albert felt the wave was both hesitant and urgent.

Rick walked over to the young man. "Did you want to talk to me about something?" he asked.

"Yes," the boy said. "I think you know my dad, Walker Farrell."

"I certainly do," Rick replied. "We met years ago at the university. Is he here today?"

"He's at home. He is sick and I think he might die. He should be in the hospital, I'm pretty sure, but my mom won't let him out of the house. She is convinced that if anyone takes him away she'll never see him again."

Rick's eyes were wide and his chin turned up. "Do you know what he is sick with? Is he throwing up or anything?"

"A doctor at the local clinic told him a couple of months ago that he has cancer. But the doctor got transferred and hasn't been replaced."

"Isn't there a nurse at the clinic?" Rick asked.

"There was but she married the doctor and left when he did. Right now there is nobody."

Rick motioned to his pilot to come with him, then asked the boy to lead him to his family home. There they met with the boy's mother and checked the pain-ridden husband. Rick called the pilot aside, spoke with him briefly, then approached the boy.

"We can get your mom and dad to Anchorage and get your dad checked into the Alaska Native Hospital, where he needs to be. We have two empty seats on our aircraft and I'll find a place for your mom to stay while she is in Anchorage. If nothing else is available she can stay at my house. Will you be OK by yourself?"

"I'll be fine," the boy said. "I'm eighteen years old."

Rick then met privately with the boy's mother, got her agreement to his plan and then waited while she hurriedly packed clothing for herself and her husband.

Rick then took Congressman Harley Whitney aside to fill him in. Whitney had been observing everything that happened since they stopped at Chena Hot Springs and nodding his approval as Rick went through the beginnings of developing his plan.

"If you don't mind," he said, "we will be overnighting in Fairbanks. I have some friends I'd like you to meet, we could have a nice dinner at one of my favorite restaurants and our pilots will be back here first thing in the morning to resume our journey."

Harley laughed. "I would be delighted to spend a night in Fairbanks and meet your friends," he said. "Our aircraft and its pilots are needed for a mission of mercy. Please, send them on their way."

THE PILOTS DID INDEED RETURN THE FOLLOWING DAY and the group resumed their trip.On the fifth day, the Cessna crossed the rugged Brooks Range to the flat arctic plain of the North Slope and landed at Prudhoe Bay several miles from the big oil discovery made just four years earlier.

Rick Albert's pride in Alaska's abundant resources came through strongly in his descriptions of the Prudhoe Bay Field to Harley Whitney. "This is the largest discovery of crude oil ever in North America," he said as they approached the airport, "a very big deal for Alaska. Something more than 10 billion barrels of recoverable crude oil and around 26 trillion cubic feet of gas. Once a pipeline is built, if we can get approval, it will be a huge source of energy for our nation."

When the Cessna landed and taxied to a hangar, a tall and rugged man in dungarees and a sports jacket stepped out of the hangar office to greet them.

"Welcome to Prudhoe Bay," the man said, shaking their hands. "I'm Roscoe Farrell with Atlantic Petroleum, manager of this field. I don't usually greet visitors but our home office in Dallas called and said you two gentlemen were worthy of some extra effort. So here I am and I must say I am delighted to be here."

The men exchanged greetings and the field manager cheerfully led them to an oversized pickup truck, loaded them inside and began an extensive tour of America's latest and greatest major oil discovery.

Whitney was impressed by everything he saw. It was still early October but the ground was already covered with snow. And pawing their way to the tundra plants below were large herds of caribou.

"I'm surprised that the wild caribou come so close to the drilling rigs and the people that work there," he said.

"Yes," Farrell replied. "We've been surprised by that ourselves. I asked Angus Gavin, the ecologist doing wildlife surveys for the companies about it. He told me the caribou's greatest enemies are the wolves and grizzly bears. They kill the foragers for food. But the caribou have figured out that the wolves and bears are afraid of the people and stay away, so the caribou gravitate to the tundra near human operations because they are safe from the predators there. They are most vulnerable when they're calving so the caribou gather near our rigs when that time draws near."

"That's not what we hear from the people opposed to oil development and construction of the pipeline."

"I know," Farrell said. "They tell people Alaska's oil drillers are killing and driving away the caribou. That's just not true. At calving time the spaces around the rigs become a virtual caribou maternity ward. They'll be moving out of here pretty soon now that the ground is covered with snow."

Harley Whitney had a quizzical look on his face as he filed the information away in his memory. The caribou question would be an important one if the issue of pipeline construction came before Congress.

"That couldn't happen anyplace else in Alaska," Farrell said. "South of the Brooks Range any caribou that wander near homes are likely to be shot for their meat. But the North Slope workers are not allowed to carry weapons and no hunting is allowed anywhere in the oil fields. Sometimes the safest place for caribou is as close to those oil rigs as they dare get, especially during calving season."

Whitney laughed. "I'm glad the critters have figured that out. And a little surprised. I suspect if they heard a shot, they'd all take off for the back country."

"They would indeed," Farrell replied. "If an engine backfires they get very nervous."

Chapter 38

———·———

WHEN THEIR PICKUP TRUCK REACHED PRUDHOE BAY the driver took them out a long causeway to a loading area overlooking the southern reach of the Arctic Ocean. From there if one could look over the horizon the view would be of the North Pole area and beyond, with Russia to the left and Canada to the right.

"Very impressive," he said.

Rick Albert clapped his hands together gently and gestured toward their waiting aircraft. "Fearless Leader, you have seen the industrial heart of Alaska. If you are ready we can load up, head south and take in some of the fabulous scenery along the way."

"This has been an enlightening journey," Harley said. "Alaska and Louisiana are both parts of the oil patch. But they couldn't be more different—except for the marshy ground. As I'm sure you know ours never freezes. I love my part of the country and this trip has convinced me I could love Alaska as well."

The two congressmen climbed into the Cessna, fastened their safety belts and Rick nodded to the pilot. "I think we've done as much as we can here."

The pilot turned to his control panel, fired up the engines and began taxiing to the edge of the runway. The Cessna took off, turned south toward the mountains and returned them to Anchorage. There the two congressmen enjoyed a sizable wine-fueled dinner and spent the night at the Captain Cook Hotel to get ready for a series of activities Rick had lined up for them.

THE FOLLOWING MORNING THE TWO CONGRESSMEN DROVE to the four-story office building of The Anchorage Times. Once inside they climbed a wide flight of stairs to the corporate office of the newspaper.

The publisher's secretary, Dorothy Beaulieu, met them at the top of the stairs and led them into Atwood's office. Bob Atwood leaped from behind his desk with a wide smile on his face and grabbed Whitney's hand, then turned for a vigorous shake with Rick Albert.

"Welcome to our fair city, Harley Whitney," he said. "We are delighted to have you here. And Rick, welcome back and thank you for bringing Harley to Alaska. I wish every member of Congress could come and see what Alaska is all about. They make a lot of decisions that have major impacts on our state and need to be as well educated on it as you are becoming. Please take a seat. Can I get you something to drink?"

"A glass of water would go down nicely right now," Whitney said. "And I'm looking forward to having something a little stronger when we come to your lawn party this evening. It was very nice of you to arrange that. I hope it won't be too much of an imposition on your family."

"Oh no," Atwood said, "we love to entertain and have been fortunate to be able to build our house on what once was a golf course. The vistas are wide and the view is incredible. From one side or the house you have the wide reach of Cook Inlet before you and Mount McKinley in the distance. We have invited a bunch of people that Rick and I and my wife Evangeline thought you would want to meet."

"I look forward to it," Harley said. "I'm sure it will be a highlight of my trip."

A DRIVER ARRIVED AT THE CAPTAIN COOK promptly at 5:20 that evening to take the two congressmen to the party at Atwood's estate, which no longer resembled a golf course. "This is the most impressive house in Alaska," Rick Albert told Harley as they approached. "And I think you will enjoy his friends. They include the leaders in both the business and civic communities of Alaska and more."

Harley nodded. "Alaska is a unique place," he said, and that includes the grand scenery, the tall mountains, water bodies like Cook Inlet and it certainly includes the people. Thank you for bringing me here. It is the trip of a lifetime."

The driver dropped them at the end of the long sidewalk leading to Atwood's home and asked them to call his office when they were ready to go back to the hotel.

The reception was as promised with more than a hundred of Alaska's leaders, both men and women, and their spouses, roaming the large Atwood lawn with drinks in hand. Whitney noted that many of the leaders, people with impressive jobs and titles, were women. That was something unique about Alaska, something rarely seen in much of the country.

Just before 8 p.m. Bob Atwood rapped his wine glass against a large glass bowl and asked for attention.

"Thank you all for coming," he said. "Before we adjourn for the evening I just wanted to give Harley Whitney my thanks for coming to Alaska and for coming tonight to meet you fine people. Alaska has a great destiny and those here for this occasion are the ones who will have an important role to play in meeting the challenges ahead. Congress has some critical decisions to make that will have a major impact on Alaska, the trans-Alaska oil pipeline being just one. My fond hope is that Congressman Whitney will remember his trip here, the things he has seen and the people he has met when it comes time to vote."

"I will indeed," Whitney said as the crowd erupted in cheers and enthusiastic applause.

At that point the crowd began to disperse and Rick Albert walked into the Atwood mansion to call their driver. Twenty minutes later the driver arrived, Harley Whitney said his goodbyes and Rick led him to the waiting vehicle.

"A great night," Whitney said to Rick as they buckled in and the driver looked around before driving off toward their hotel. "Where to next?" he asked.

"Juneau," Rick replied. "Governor Gruening called and is back from a trip to Seattle. He would love to meet with us if we can get there. I suggest we head to Southeast Alaska in the morning."

"Let's do it."

Chapter 39

THE NEXT AFTERNOON GEORGE TALLENT was driving to work at the Alaska State Troopers' Anchorage Detachment and listening to the car radio. As he turned into the office driveway an announcer broke into the music program with an urgent message:

"The Federal Aviation Administration reports that a light plane on its way from Anchorage to Juneau has disappeared somewhere en route. Aboard the missing aircraft are Alaska Congressman Rick Albert, U.S. House Majority Leader Harley Whitney and two other men. Apparently one of the two is an aide to Congressman Albert and the fourth is the plane's owner and pilot, Donald Walker. We'll provide more on this developing story as we get it."

Tallent jammed on his brakes, swerved to the side of the road and sat stunned behind the wheel. Rick Albert was not only his closest friend but one of the most important political figures in Alaska. And Harley Whitney was one of the nation's leading politicians. Tallent drove quickly to a parking spot and trotted into the building.He was greeted at the door by Lieutenant Ralph Worthen, commander of the statewide Criminal Investigation Bureau, which was headquartered in the Anchorage Detachment office.

"Congressman Rick Albert has disappeared," Worthen said, urgency in his voice, "and House Majority Leader Harley Whitney is with him. We need to see if there is anything suspicious about it. Could be an accident somewhere along the route and they might turn up yet, but search and ground crews are headed out to scour the area. Everyone is worried. See what you can find out."

"I'm on it," Tallent said, and headed for his desk. He flipped open his phone directory and dialed a contact at the Federal Aviation Administration.

The FAA man recognized Tallent's voice. "George," the man said, "this could be bad. The plane is overdue in Juneau by more than an hour and nobody has heard from them, at least as far as we know. The pilot is Don Fallon of Anchorage and Albert's aide Roger Tubert is also on board. Fallon filed a flight plan under visual flight rules but the weather along the way called for stiff headwinds, marginal visibility and freezing rain. They shouldn't have been flying in that crap. No telling what happened."

"What was the route?" Tallent asked. "Could they be stopped at an airfield along the way?"

"Not likely. They went through Portage Pass to Prince William Sound and were headed south from there to Juneau. Yakutat is the only spot they could land without floats and the plane is on wheels. We checked Yakutat. You know the place; it's just a small airfield at the head of the Inside Passage, and they aren't there. The flight to Juneau ordinarily takes three and a half hours but they left here more than five hours ago. The last weather report indicated there was a 700-foot ceiling at Yakutat with a mile and a half of visibility and low fog. We don't know if they made it that far. The last radio contact we had they were about ten miles south of Portage Pass. We're scrambling military and civilian aircraft, anything available, and will be searching the water and shoreline along the entire route. If they haven't landed somewhere that plane could be down anywhere between Anchorage and Juneau."

"Did the plane have an emergency locator beacon?" Tallent asked.

"Good question," the FAA man said. "Fallon, the pilot, was supposed to install a brand new one in the aircraft a week ago. But so far none of the search planes has picked up a signal from the Gulf of Alaska. And the FAA says its tower in Fairbanks is getting a signal from a Cessna parked at the airport there. It's apparently the one registered to Albert's pilot. Fallon might have sold his to a guy there and hasn't installed the new one yet. We just don't know. The law requiring the beacons is new and not all the pilots are following it. Some pilots buy the things and install them when they get around to it."

Tallent paused for a thought, then asked: "Do you know anything about Fallon?"

"I see him sometimes when I stop at the Glacier Tavern after work. He's kind of a regular there."

"Thanks Chris," Tallent said. "I'll see what I can find out. Let me know if you hear anything."

Tallent hung up the phone, stuck his head into Lieutenant Worthen's office and said: "I'm headed down to the Glacier Tavern. Got a tip that Rick Albert's pilot hangs around there." Worthen grimly nodded his agreement.

George parked his cruiser at the edge of the tavern's small parking lot. Leaving it close to the door might signal to customers and passersby that a State Trooper in uniform was in the Glacier on official business. He wanted to avoid attention. The customers would see him but the distant vehicle would make the visit seem more casual, perhaps a drink after work.

The tavern was a dimly-lit establishment with many years of usage obvious in its faded paint job and dusty light fixtures. Though it was still early evening, a small crowd had already begun to fill up the booths and barstools. George's quiet entrance drew many turned heads, though all seemed just mildly curious about the uniformed officer and which of their colleagues he might be visiting.

He approached the bartender, who was wiping some newly washed drink glasses. "I understand Don Fallon is one of your regulars," George said.

The bartender dropped his dishrag into a sink and replied: "He is."

"Have you seen him lately?"

The bartender grimaced. "He was in here last night, stayed a few hours. Mind if I ask why you want to know?"

Rick's face became pensive. "I can't tell you that right now. What was he drinking?"

"Don is fond of boilermakers, a glass of beer with a whiskey shooter."

The State Trooper pulled a notebook from his shirt pocket. "How many did he have?"

"I'm not sure," the bartender answered. "He was with a couple of other guys and they ordered a number of times. Maybe four or five. Also ate a bunch of snacks—popcorn and potato chips."

"Who were the other guys?"

The bartender hesitated, then replied: "One guy I didn't know but the other one was Vinnie Matusi. He's sitting in that back booth eating his lunch if you want to talk to him."

George pocketed his notebook and approached the man in the rear booth, a grizzled character who looked to be in his 60s. He knew that Matusi was a member of the Alaska underworld but could also be a valuable source of information. "Vinnie," he said, "can we talk for a minute?"

The man hesitated, then gestured to the seat opposite him. "Put 'er there. What's up?"

"Were you here last night with Don Fallon?"

"Yeah, we had a few." A worried look crossed Matusi's face. "He didn't crack up that airplane of his, did he?"

"I'm not sure what happened," Tallent replied. "He's missing and he might be hurt. Just trying to figure out where he might be."

"Wow," Matusi said. "He's a pilot. That could be bad."

Tallent made a notation in his pad and asked: "Did you go anywhere after you left here?"

"On the way home we stopped and had a couple at the Nevada Grill."

"Same thing you drank here?"

"Yeah," Matusi replied. "I had a couple of scotches on the rocks and Don always drinks boilermakers. He likes those things. I can't handle all the beer. Makes me have to get up to piss in the middle of the night. Then I can't get back to sleep."

George thanked the man, left and drove to the Nevada Grill on the south side of the city. It was even seedier than the Glacier Tavern and its booths and tables were still lightly occupied. Its clientele tended to gather late in the evening after most people had finished dinner and restaurants were emptying out.

The Nevada's day manager phoned his night bartender and confirmed that Fallon and Matusi had been there after midnight and Fallon had several boilermakers, though he couldn't remember how many. It had been a busy time in the grill.

Chapter 40

WHEN TALLENT RETURNED TO HIS OFFICE, Lieutenant Worthen called him into his office.

"Anything new on the aircraft?" George asked.

"No," Worthen said, "search planes are all over that route but no sign of the Cessna. Did you learn anything?"

"Yeah," Tallent answered. "the pilot spent the evening and a couple hours after midnight at a couple of downtown bars. It sounds like he drank quite a few boilermakers, enough to give most people a snoot-full."

"Hmm," the lieutenant said. "That's not good. Unless we can find him, dead or alive, there is no way to know how much alcohol was in his system. Boozing that soon before flying seems like a dangerous business."

Tallent shook his head woefully. "How is Rick's family doing?"

"They're scared to death, as you can imagine. Myrlie is convinced the plane has crashed and her husband is dead. You and your wife Cindy are pretty close to Rick and Myrlie, as I remember"

"Oh yeah, we go way back. Ever since high school. Cindy is worried sick."

"I'm not a praying man," Lieutenant Worthen said, "but I'll keep my fingers crossed for you both. Rick Albert has done a lot of good things for Alaska. For himself, as well, but he has brought a lot of federal money to Alaska and he's done right by the state.

The House Majority Leader is with him. He is one of the most important people in Washington."

"I'm going to go back to my office and do a little noodling and head-scratching," Tallent replied.

"Have at it," Worthen called to George's' retreating figure.

"But first," George thought to himself, "I'm going to check out the route they flew."

George drove to Anchorage International Airport, then took a road skirting the east side of the airport to the State Trooper hangar. There he checked out a twin-engine Cessna, climbed into the cockpit and ran the engine until its temperature indicated it was ready for takeoff. He called the Anchorage Tower, got permission to taxi to the foot of the runway, then started his takeoff and his journey.

Once in the air he turned south and flew along Turnagain Arm to a pass near the village of Portage, then crossed through the mountains to the Gulf of Alaska. As the Cessna entered the airspace of the Gulf, George spotted an unusual glint from the water surface below. He flew in a relatively tight circle and dropped the plane lower as he approached the spot from the opposite direction. A small area near the entrance to Portage Pass appeared to be covered by a sheen of oil. George made a mental note of what he saw and recrossed the area looking for wreckage. He saw none but continued looking, anxious to find some sign of his lifelong friend. Two commercial fishing boats were within about five miles of the spot and could have been the source of the oil sheen, perhaps and perhaps not.

After crisscrossing the northwestern edge of the Gulf of Alaska near Portage he decided to play a hunch and swung left over the frozen surface of Columbia Glacier. The sun was bright and the reflection from the glacier's white surface made vision difficult. To avoid missing anything he reversed course, then began a series of sweeps over the glacier surface. As his search progressed George was struck by an eery feeling that his friend was somewhere in the vast ice and snow vista below him. He saw nothing to confirm it; the feeling was intensely personal. Because of it he continued his long series of sweeps, his eyes riveted to the cockpit window and the white mass below. The feeling never left him but when he saw that his fuel gauge indicated it was time to return to Anchorage he reluctantly turned back toward Portage Pass and returned to Anchorage.

The strange conviction that Rick Albert and the others lay somewhere in, on or under Columbia Glacier stuck with him so George vowed that he would search the surface of the glacier. It was an unlikely place for the aircraft and its passengers to be since it was not even on a direct line between Portage and Juneau. It was always possible that the aircraft had diverted from its route but there was no information suggesting that it had done so. George was determined to search the surface and see for sure if there was any sign of the aircraft or its occupants on the glacier ice. He knew that if the aircraft were on the surface it would have been quickly covered by snow, especially if it had fallen into one of the glacier's many crevasses.

THAT EVENING HE VENTED HIS GROWING FRUSTRATION to his wife Cindy. "That plane has got to be down out there somewhere," he said. "But there's no sign of it. None. The Air Force has looked everywhere with no luck. They've even taken photographs of the entire surface. I think the plane is somewhere on the bottom of the Gulf of Alaska," he said, "but I'm stumped on where to look next.

George spent the next day at his desk calling people in communities along Turnagain Arm and on the shoreline around Prince William Sound. He made a dozen calls to people who might have seen it from their home or office windows, but found no one who had seen the missing plane on its flight path. The official search party continued its efforts for another week but eventually gave up in frustration.

Chapter 41

———◆———

THE FOLLOWING WEEKS BECAME EXTREMELY FRUSTRATING for Investigator George Tallent. The search for the missing aircraft was intense and continued all along the expected route of the Cessna. The searchers were led by 40 Air Force craft including several spy planes with intense-resolution cameras that could photograph the ocean thousands of feet below their wings. The searchers found nothing, no wreckage, no oil slicks, no signs that an aircraft might be hidden nearby, buried in snow on the glacier or sunken in seawater a thousand feet deep or more. After 39 days of fruitless flights over the open water and beach areas of the Gulf of Alaska from Portage to Juneau, the search was determined to be fruitless and suspended pending any new information. On December 29 a court declared the four men to be dead. The declaration enabled their families to begin scheduling church services and settling their estates.

At his supervisor's suggestion, George began checking every rumor and report of related information that might suggest criminal action. As time passed and the story of the missing plane was repeated by the nation's news media, reports began coming in of people who dreamed about the aircraft and where it might be lying or heard rumors about acquaintances who might be involved. Running them down seemed a terrible waste of time and energy, but the Alaska Troopers could afford to overlook no possibility. Tallent did almost all of the work by phone since none of the tips seemed likely to be related to the case itself.

One grim item surfaced when a source called Tallent with the news that a suspicious character had been sighted near the hangar where Don Fallon's Cessna was stored. The man was in the area the night before the flight and was confronted by a maintenance worker. He had claimed he was thinking of chartering a Cessna-421 and just wondered what they looked like. Said his wife would be coming with him and she is very fussy.

"Did they get the guy's name?" Tallent asked.

"No, it didn't seem important at the time," the man said. "They just wanted to keep him away from Fallon's plane. I can give you the maintenance man's contact information if that will help. The guy is at Merrill Field right now if you want to run by there."

Tallent jumped into his vehicle and headed for the small airport immediately. He found the maintenance worker and interviewed him at length. The man gave a detailed description of the character and Tallent wrote down the information.

"What made you suspicious about the guy?" he asked. "I assume a lot of people come through the area. This is a busy little airport."

The maintenance worker shrugged. "Might be nothing but he was peering into the back of Don Fallon's aircraft. He told me he was trying to figure out if his wife would be comfortable in it on a long flight."

"Did you have reason to disbelieve him?"

"No, it made sense to me. There are no toilets on these small planes, just jugs and bedpans that can be uncomfortable to use. Most people just try to hold it in until they land."

Tallent returned to his office and wrote notes on the incident but it seemed an unpromising lead.

DESPITE BEING MISSING AND PROBABLY DEAD, Congressman Rick Albert handily won re-election in November. The voters were unable to accept the possibility that their candidate would not be back, and many voted for him simply as a final tribute.

The Alaska Legislature appointed one of their own members to take the seat, State Senator Don Young. Young would be officially elected to the U.S. House seat in a special election held the following year and staked claim to what he hoped would be a long political career.

As Christmas of 1972 neared, the nation's attention shifted to more seasonal concerns and the search for the missing congressmen in the southern portion of Alaska continued but at a much less intense pace. Gradually the world became accustomed to the likelihood that the two high-profile politicians and their companions might be lost forever and their true fate would never be known.

TALLENT WAS EXHAUSTED BY THE INTENSE INVESTIGATION and its climax so he and Cindy took a well-earned month-long vacation, spending much of it in Hawaii before heading to Seattle for the last few days. There they visited friends and George spent two days at the University of Washington developing information on research capabilities in the area.

When their return flight landed in Anchorage they were met at the terminal by Lieutenant Gilmour.

Tallent laughed. "Are you just welcoming us home or do you have a new assignment for me?"

"Both," Gilmour replied.

"Can you give me any details on the assignment?" George asked.

"I will when you get in the office. I just wanted to make sure you were going to be around."

"You bet," George said. "I'll be there in a few days."

"No rush."

Chapter 42

----·----

TALLENT TOOK A LONG-WEEKEND VACATION before returning to work. He was still exhausted by the emotional impact of the long investigation into the Bush Company murders and anxious to return to more mundane matters, though boredom in the life of an Alaska State Trooper was rarely a problem.

Lieutenant Worthen welcomed him, thanked George for his work on the Bush Company case and said: "In case you were wondering, we still have nothing on the disappearance of our congressman and the majority leader of the U.S. House. A whole fleet of light aircraft has combed every beach, wooded area and mountainside between Anchorage and Juneau, but there is no sign of them or their aircraft. I suspect the plane and its four occupants are at the bottom of the Gulf of Alaska somewhere. And that thing is five miles deep in some places. The airplane might never be found."

"Thanks, lieutenant," Tallent replied. "I guess it's pretty hopeless but Rick was my best friend and we hung out together for many years. I may get over losing him someday, but I suspect that won't be for a very long time."

"I think I know how you feel," the lieutenant said. "I've lost friends but never in a deal like this one. If you need any vacation time, let me know. And if you want to do some more traveling and want to borrow a few bucks, I'd be glad to kick in and wouldn't need to get it back for a long time, if ever."

Tallent shook his head sadly. "That would just give me more time to think," he said. "The best thing would probably be just to get back to work and try to keep my mind off it."

"There is one thing that came up about the pilot of Albert's plane," Worthen said. "Don Fallon is his name and he is, as you know, something of a boozer. But it turns out he might also be an overconfident pilot. There is an article by him in this month's Aviation magazine. One of the things he says in the piece is that icing is manageable and a skilled pilot can do work-arounds that let you fly in almost any kind of weather. If that's the way he thinks, I wouldn't fly with him even if he did turn up alive somewhere."

Tallent borrowed Worthen's copy of Aviation magazine and read the Don Fallon article carefully. Many of the words suggested Fallon was a knowledgeable pilot but several passages virtually reeked with overconfidence. Tallent read one sentence intently, closed the magazine and pondered Fallon's unbelievable words:

"If you are sneaky, smart and careful, you can fly 350 days a year and disregard 99 per cent of the b.s. you hear about icing."

The thought crossed the trooper's mind that the aircraft bearing the remains of the two congressmen and their two associates were almost certainly at the bottom of the Gulf of Alaska somewhere between Portage and Juneau, probably nearer the northern segment where the Weather Bureau had reported sporadic heavy rain with significant icing conditions the morning of their flight. The bureau even issued a warning to pilots operating in the area.

"Good grief!" he said to himself.

The thought of his buddy Rick and the others sitting forever in a plane at the bottom of the Gulf of Alaska haunted George. He decided he needed to get away from work for a few days. George and his wife Cindy were both avid downhill skiers. They spent many weekends at the ski resort south of Anchorage and stayed at a friend's cabin whenever the friend wasn't using it. The man, Walter Anderson, was a pilot for Alaska Airlines who spent much of his time traveling. He was a kind and generous person who held both George and Cindy in high regard, considering it a privilege when he could offer the cabin to his Trooper buddy and his wife. Their presence also provided a high degree of security against anyone seeking to break in and rob the cabin, which was generally available for George and Cindy at least two or three weekends per month through the winter. Leaving a cabin empty can be an invitation to trouble.

ONE THURSDAY IN EARLY DECEMBER CINDY ROSE while they were watching television, stretched her arms and told George: "Let's get some skiing in this weekend. We haven't been on the mountain in weeks and I could use some exercise. What do you think?"

George stared at her ample and well-formed bosom, smiled and replied: "You make a very persuasive argument. Walt said he was going to be off flying until after Christmas. Let's head down there on Friday night."

Cindy laughed. "For skiing, right?"

"That too."

WHEN GEORGE GOT HOME AFTER WORK ON FRIDAY, Cindy had their skis, winter clothes and the rest of their gear packed. "You really want to head to Girdwood, don't you?"

"We're all ready," she said. "Change your clothes and let's get out of here."

"How about dinner?"

"I could cook something but I was thinking we might have dinner at the lodge restaurant."

"Sounds good to me."

They drove to Girdwood and its Alyeska Resort, requested the key at the front desk and settled in at their friend's nicely appointed condominium. After unpacking their gear they went to the resort's signature restaurant and were assigned a choice table overlooking the Girdwood Valley, one with an outstanding view of the night sky. The food was excellent and on their way out they encountered the resort manager, Chris Stockard.

"Yo, Chris!" George said. "How goes it."

"Hi George, Cindy. Great to see you. It's going just fine. Been a very busy week. Lots of skiers in from town and a large group that flew in from Seattle. They have a meeting of some kind and are keeping the kitchen and bar staffs hopping."

"Ka-ching!" George said with a laugh, faking the sound of a cash register.

"You betcha, my friend. What's good for Alyeska is good for Anchorage."

"Way to go. Hope it keeps up."

"Been a great season so far."

George and Cindy went to their room and opened a bottle of wine before their night of love, which kept them awake and active until the early morning.

Around four a.m. they were awakened by a knock at the door. George threw on a bathrobe and opened the door. It was the hotel manager.

"There has been a robbery," the man said. "And I think Chris Stockard has been shot, badly hurt. His wife just called. He had the week's proceeds in a bag in his cabin. You need to get down there."

George looked back at Cindy. "You go," she said. "Take the car and let me know what's happening when you can."

George dressed hurriedly, raced out to the parking lot, started his family car and spun out onto the access road, pulling up in front of the Stockard family cabin. Nancy Stockard ran out of the house and thew her arms around him, obviously terrified.

"Is Chris OK?" he asked.

"He's hurt," she said, "but he's alert and talking. The robber shot him in the shoulder. The Anchorage Fire Department is sending an ambulance to take him to Providence Hospital."

George ran to the cabin's front door where the haggard resort manager met him, his face white and his shirt red with blood.

"I'm OK, I think. It hurts like hell but it seems like something that can be fixed. The ambulance crew will be here in a minute. You get after that bastard who made off with my proceeds briefcase."

"What did he look like?" George asked.

"Maybe late thirties. Short, medium build. Beard and mustache. Had on a gray parka and a green ski hat. He can't be too far away; took off about fifteen minutes ago."

George suggested the manager sit down and await the ambulance's arrival. He could hear its siren in the distance as he raced back to his car, climbed in and raced off down the road toward the main highway. George reached the highway just as the ambulance made its turn onto the resort road, lights and siren blazing.

As he approached the highway a man ran out from the adjacent Chevron station and waved to George's speeding car.

George slammed on his brakes and rolled down his window as the uniformed station manager ran huffing toward him. "I don't know what that guy has been up to," he said, "but he came racing down from the resort and smashed into my wife's car. Then he took off down the highway south toward the mountains."

George thanked the man, rolled up his window and sped off south into the mountain-flanked core of the Kenai Peninsula. Five miles from the Girdwood turnoff the road veers away from the adjacent railroad tracks and takes a steep turn into the mountains. As George approached he could see a wrecked car off the road by the turn. He climbed out and found the vehicle empty but with boot tracks running out to the railroad tracks and disappearing into the snow to the south. He took off in pursuit of the fleeing man, afoot and an unknown distance behind his prey.

George plodded doggedly through the snow for more than an hour and could still see foot tracks but no sign of the robber. He heard the sound of an approaching locomotive and turned to see a train drawing near and slowing down. George pulled his badge from a pocket and flashed it at the passing engineer. The trainman waved and applied his brakes, bringing the train to a halt about fifty yards past him.

George climbed aboard and hastily described the situation to the engineer.

"I'll be glad to help," he man said. "These things aren't designed to chase crooks but we'll give her a go."

"Thanks," George said. "Much appreciated."

Fifteen minutes later the train rounded a wide turn and the engineer spotted a man beside the tracks waving for the trainman to stop for him. The man fit the description of the robber given by the wounded manager at Alyeska Resort. His arms were wrapped tightly around his body and he was obviously very cold.

"What do you want me to do?" the engineer asked George.

"Why give the poor man a ride, if you don't mind stopping again."

The trainman smiled, nodded and applied his brakes once more while George stepped back out of sight in the engine's cab. As the train slowed and came to a stop the man on the tracks ran over and began climbing aboard. As he reached the top of the ladder he reached inside his pocket.

George stepped forward, stuck a pistol barrel in the man's ear and said: "Don't even think about it." He removed a pistol from the man's pocket and slipped handcuffs onto his wrists. George and his prisoner stayed on the train until its next stop, where two State Troopers in a patrol car waited to take custody of the handcuffed robber.

Chapter 43

T ALLENT SPENT THE BALANCE OF THE WEEKEND with Cindy in a cottage at Big Lake north of Anchorage. On Monday he went back to work with a vengeance and spent the next few years working on a series of major cases. He was eventually promoted to captain and spent much of his time supervising other investigators. He retired in 1992 when he became eligible after twenty years of service. Tallent then took a job selling real estate and was quite successful in both the residential and commercial property markets in and around Anchorage. His intelligence and affability were genuine assets in the job and prospective clients appreciated his knowledge of the regional market and of the state of Alaska in general.

The sales commissions were sizable but the State of Alaska offered generous retirement benefits, including comprehensive medical coverage, so he didn't really need the additional income from real estate sales. The job was actually just an antidote to the boredom of retirement but there were better ways, especially for people with the right skills.

Tallent approached Worthen, who by then was a major, and made a special request. George told Worthen he wanted to do police work again, returning as a cold case investigator, a special detective's assignment that involved delving into cases that had gone unsolved for years and the officers originally assigned to the case had given up and gone on to other matters. Because the cases were cold and clues were few, most cold case investigations were handled by retirees who had greater control of how they spent their time and where they focused it. The cases were also problematic since those who did the original investigations were often defensive about their work and their conclusions. Some active-duty officers complained loudly about the work of the cold-case teams, but Alaska State Trooper management understood their value and supported them solidly at budget time.

George worked on cold cases primarily from his home though he had access to the AST complex and was especially drawn to the state crime laboratory on Martin Luther King Jr. Avenue in Anchorage. The lab was a state-of-the-art facility with skilled technicians and the ability to draw on support and assistance from a wide variety of state and federal offices.

His first day on the job Major Worthen called and asked him to look into a request from the Sears department store headquarters in Illinois.

"What's up?" Tallent asked.

"The company's store in Anchorage got a call from a local woman who found a $250 gift certificate issued by the store fifteen years ago."

"Was it stolen?"

"Yes, it was in the cash register at a liquor store in Muldoon when it was robbed years back. Somebody apparently used it to buy booze and the clerk took it for a big discount figuring he could make money reselling it."

"What happened to it."

"Some guy walked into the store, pulled a pistol and demanded all the money in the register. The clerk was terrified and froze but was cooperating when an Anchorage police officer walked by, looked in the window and noticed that the clerk talking to a customer had a very strained look on his face. The cop decided to check the situation out and entered the store. The clerk looked up and turned his head when he saw the uniformed officer coming through the door. The robber noticed the man's shift of attention, turned to the officer and shot him. He fell dead in the doorway"

"What about the clerk?" Tallent asked.

"He was reaching under the counter for his own pistol when the hood turned back, guessed what he was doing and shot him too. The cop and the clerk were both fatalities. The robber scooped up everything in the register, all but the coins, and took off out the door."

"The guy was apparently wearing gloves," Worthen added. "There were no unidentifiable prints on the cash register or anywhere else in the store, nothing that pointed to a shooter."

"What about *identifiable* fingerprints."

"The store clerk's were all over the gift certificate. That was definitely the one from the robbery."

"So where did the woman find the gift certificate?" Tallent asked.

"It was in her boyfriend's bureau drawer."

"Do we know anything about the boyfriend?"

"He has a record for robbery and petty theft. Did time in prison, but not a lot."

"Thanks Major, I'm on it."

Tallent went through the file on the woman's boyfriend. The man was obviously a tough guy whose time in the state penitentiary was marked by frequent transgressions. He was prone to violence and engaged in numerous fistfights, some of which added time to his existing sentences.

The woman was then working as a waitress in a restaurant in Downtown Anchorage. He went to her workplace in civilian clothes, sat at one of her tables and introduced himself when she came to take his order.

"What do you want?" she asked.

"I'd like to know more about your boyfriend and that gift certificate you found in his belongings. I take it you know a little about how he came by it."

"Not much," she said. "I'd like to talk to you but I can't right now. I'm very busy. Could you come by when I get off at four and I'll meet you in the coffee shop next door."

Tallent nodded, opened his wallet and left a bill to cover the cost of his soft drink and a large tip. He was waiting in a booth at the coffee shop when she entered shortly after four. He waved and she walked to meet him and slid into the booth opposite him.

"Thank you for coming," he said. "Do you know anything about how Nate came to have that Sears gift certificate in his sock drawer."

The woman grimaced knowing that life was about to get more complicated for her boyfriend. "No," she said quietly. "It has been there for a long time. I've seen it many times and I finally decided to see if it was worth anything. Was it stolen?"

Tallent nodded and placed his hands on the table. "Yes," he said, "it was taken in a robbery at a Muldoon liquor store fifteen years ago. A police officer walked into the store while the robbery was in progress. The robber shot him and then the clerk, killed them both."

"Yikes," she said, a horrified look crossing her face. "Nate is a tough guy but I never imagined he could do anything like that. I do know that he was in a very difficult situation some years back before we met. He was a nervous wreck for a long time. But he has been a pretty solid citizen for as long as I've known him. Never been in trouble, not even small stuff."

"It was a terrible crime," Tallent said. "Both the police officer and the clerk were married and had young kids. The youngsters are now all in college, I believe, but they had to grow up without their dads. Their mothers raised them and worked to earn money for college. Fortunately the kids are bright and won a few scholarships."

"That is just terrible news," the woman said. "Nate a murderer and a robber? You just can't tell about some people. Is there anything I can do to help the families? I don't have much but maybe I could help a little with college expenses."

"I'll find that out and give you their addresses. The police officer's family is pretty well taken care of but I understand the clerk's family is in somewhat difficult straits. The wife could probably use some help. And keep in mind there is a possibility the robber wasn't Nate," George said. "It was a long time ago and the gift certificate disappeared in the robbery but we don't know where it has been since then. Nate might have gotten it from somebody else, perhaps the guy who robbed the liquor store and killed those two people. I need to talk to him about it. We also need to get the gift certificate and run some tests on it."

"I have the certificate here in my purse. And Nate is at the apartment now if you want to go by there."

"Does he have any weapons?"

"A pistol he keeps in that sock drawer. But I've never seen him take it out."

"Where is the sock drawer?"

"Top right drawer in the bureau. In the bedroom on the right. Be gentle with him if you can. He is a pretty good man, at least these days."

Tallent thanked the woman, excused himself and left the coffee shop. He went home to put on his uniform and then drove to the address she had given him. He climbed the stairs to the third-floor apartment and knocked on the door.

The door creaked narrowly open and a grizzled face peered out.

"Nate Parker, I'm Trooper George Tallent. I'd like to talk to you."

"What about?"

"About a robbery and double murder that took place fifteen years ago in Muldoon."

"I don't know nothin' about that," he said.

"May I come in?"

"Uh, yeah. Just let me get a shirt out of the bedroom."

Tallent pushed open the door and stepped quickly ahead of the man. He opened the bedroom door, moved to the bureau and opened the top right drawer. There in a corner was a pistol, which he pulled out and showed to the suspect.

"Is this yours?" he asked.

"Yeah, I'm old enough. What's the problem."

"You are a convicted felon in possession of a concealable

firearm. I know there is a state law against that and it might be a federal violation as well."

"Oh shit," the man said.

"Yes, indeed," Tallent replied. "You could say that."

George handcuffed the man, threw a jacket over his shoulders and led him outside to his car parked at the curb. He drove him to Anchorage Police Headquarters, asked the officers there to put him in a holding cell, then left and drove to the State Crime Lab. There he took a seat until a technician came out to meet him in the waiting room, the expert with whom Tallent left the gift certificate after receiving it from the woman.

"Were there any fingerprints on the certificate?" he asked.

The technician nodded. "Well, you already knew that Nate Parker's prints were on it and his girlfriend's as well. There was another small partial print that we were wondering about but it was too small to do anything with using our technology. The feds have new equipment that can read even the tiny partials. A report came back on that partial print this morning. It was left by the clerk in that liquor store years ago, the one who got shot along with the police officer."

George smiled and rubbed his hands together. "That ties it up," he told the technician. "Parker was the guy who robbed that store and killed both the cop and the clerk before he took off with the cash and the gift certificate."

"There's more," the lab man said. "The .38 you found in his bureau drawer is the one used in the two murders. For some reason he hung onto it even though it ties him directly to the killings."

"Too cheap to dump it and buy another one. He hung onto it. Such stupidity happens sometimes. The guys who pull these crimes aren't always the brightest cats in town. If I were you I would bust his ass as soon as possible and hang him out to dry."

George nodded. "You can count on that," he said. "Thanks for your help."

George jogged back to his car and drove to Police Headquarters. There he checked in at the holding area and was led to a gray cell that somehow seemed colder than the actual room temperature.

"Mr. Parker," he said, "that gift certificate you've been hanging on to for all these years was stolen in a robbery twenty-five years ago."

"Oh shit," Parker said.

George grimaced. "It gets worse than that. Two people were killed in that robbery, a clerk and a police officer who wandered into the store while the robbery was in progress. We have reason to believe that you committed both the robbery and the murders. So you'll be moving out of this facility and will be transferred to a holding area in the Alaska State Trooper Headquarters building on the south side of the city."

"I already have a call in to a lawyer," Parker said, his face pale. "I'd like to call him back and tell him to get his ass over here."

"You might want to have him meet you at AST Headquarters," George said. "I'm sure he knows the way."

When George checked in at his office in the Trooper Headquarters building, Major Worthen congratulated him on his handling of the old Muldoon robbery and murder case. "Great way to start your cold-case career," he said with a broad smile on his face.

Chapter 44

———

GEORGE'S NEW CAREER INVOLVED CONSIDERABLE TRAVEL, as he knew it would. Much of it was to areas of Alaska he rarely visited, an aspect of the job that he greatly enjoyed, though the circumstances of his visit weren't always enjoyable.

In the spring of 1970 a woman in California called the Ketchikan Police Department complaining that her son, Scott Woburn, had been missing near the Southeast Alaska city for twenty years and she was certain that his wife, Jane Wrath, had killed him. Ketchikan officers had investigated the case when the man was first reported missing and concluded that he simply ran away from Jane. They visited the cabin where the California couple had been living but could find no sign of a murder. The wife insisted that her husband, then thirty years old, had run away with another woman. She was sure of it.

The man's mother kept calling and was becoming something of a nuisance so the Ketchikan police had referred the matter to State Troopers hoping that would end their involvement. They considered her a hysterical and suspicious woman who didn't want to accept the most likely explanation for her son's disappearance.

Old unsolved cases were often considered a nuisance since the crimes were almost always investigated at or shortly after the time they occurred. Money had been spent on them, capable officers did the detective work and concluded it was unlikely the cases involved crimes that could be solved with a more intense effort. Those who originally investigated, if they were still available, were often defensive about their work, convinced that their earlier conclusions were the correct ones. Police agencies are chronically short of money and their investigations are more often limited by scarce financial resources than they are by lack of effort.

But Trooper George Tallent was a cautious and thorough investigator. He could keep expenses down if anyone could and had a good record for successful closure. In September of 1970, Tallent was assigned to investigate the case. He called the woman in San Diego and asked why she was convinced that her son Scott had been murdered in Ketchikan, Alaska, and why she was complaining to police twenty years after his disappearance.

"I've always been suspicious about what happened to my Scott," she replied, anguish in her voice. "Then a man named Cal Carpenter came to my house the other day. He is a pilot, what you Alaska people call bush pilots. My son's widow, a Chinese woman named Jane Wrath, took flying lessons from him and they fell in love and got married. They were living in Jane's cabin in Ketchikan, Alaska. He was Jane's second husband and he asked her one time when they were having a few drinks whatever happened to her first husband, my son Scott.

"The woman told her new husband: 'I disposed of him.' That's what she said," the man's mother sobbed. "*She disposed of him. She actually said that.*"

Tallent blinked, shook his head and asked: "How did the second husband happen to come to your house?"

"What Jane said to him got him really worried. He decided she must be nuts and that's what it would take to shoot somebody, so maybe she did it. Cal eventually left her, moved to Los Angeles and got a job. But what she said about what happened to Scott preyed on his conscience and he finally went to a priest and told him what Jane told him. The priest convinced him to do the right thing and tell the police so he came to San Diego and talked to an officer at headquarters."

"Did Jane tell him how she did it?" Tallent asked.

"She said she shot Scott in the face and the chest, then cut him up with an ax and threw his pieces into a Dumpster. She was very matter of fact about it."

"What happened to the Dumpster?"

"It was emptied into an incinerator. My Scott's body was turned to ashes with the trash."

Two days later Tallent took a two-hour flight from Anchorage to Ketchikan. He decided he needed to find some evidence, if any existed, that a man had actually been killed at Jane Wrath's cabin. In Ketchikan he took a cab to local police headquarters and briefed the officers there on his investigation. One uniformed officer took him by boat to the cabin, which was then owned by another family and had been repainted at least once over the years. With the family's permission he and the Ketchikan officer pulled up the cabin's floorboards and took samples of some soil containing a dark stain that looked a lot like blood. They scooped up a sample, replaced the floorboards and sprayed the walls with luminol, a chemical used to detect blood. Portions of the wall turned luminescent, areas where the paint had obviously been spattered with blood sometime in the cabin's history. The glowing spatter was visible through the covering paint layer. To avoid damaging the cabin walls they scraped samples from a crack that would be invisible to people using the cabin.

Tallent and the Ketchikan officer carefully cleaned the cabin floors, thanked the owners and returned to police headquarters with clear evidence that someone had been badly injured and bleeding in the building once owned by Jane Wrath and her husband. Back in Anchorage, George shipped the Ketchikan samples over to the Alaska State Crime Lab.

He asked Major Barnett to approve a trip from Anchorage to Los Angeles to interview Jane Wrath's second husband, then to San Diego to talk to Scott's mother and then on to Chicago where Jane Wrath was then living.

The major's eyes went wide. "Tallent, we don't have that much money in the budget for these cold case investigations. If we spent it on this one, there would be nothing left for other cases for the rest of the year."

George knew that the problem was real and cash was tight. Cold case detectives were expected to work mostly within the state and keep their out-of-pocket expenses low. But the Ketchikan case bugged him; he was certain he was close to figuring out what happened.

"Good grief," Barnett said, "that's a lot of expensive traveling. Can't you do any of it by phone."

"I'd much rather meet with each of them in person," George replied. "I need to see their eyes and the look on their face when they are answering my questions. And the longest leg of the trip is from Anchorage to Seattle. Once I get there I can make shorter trips between the three cities and save money over what it would cost to make separate trips over a few months—and maybe spread it over two budget cycles.

"The suspect is ready to talk, I think. She's already telling other people. This looks like a murder that has been covered up as a disappearance. It has been bugging the man's widow for twenty years. And she just blurted it out. When her second husband asked about his predecessor, she said she 'disposed of him.' I talked to the second husband on the phone and apparently he didn't press her on the issue. He just casually asked whatever happened to Scott and she told him. If she told him I think she'll tell me, but I need to be face-to-face when I ask her."

"I'm sorry, George," the major said. "The money just isn't there."

Tallent went back to his office and stewed about the dilemma. He grabbed a phone and called his old friend in Washington, Congressman Don Young.

"Can you do me a favor, Don. The department here has virtually zero budget for travel expenses but I'm working on a murder case and am very close to breaking it. The problem is I need to get to Seattle and do some traveling around to cities like Los Angeles and Seattle."

"How much do you need?"

"A couple of thousand would probably do it, but it you have a good source you could tap I'd ask for five thousand. That would allow me and the other guy currently working cold cases to do a little traveling when we need to."

Young laughed. "How about I call Vinnie DiMaggio? He is finance chairman in the Alaska House and an old friend of mine."

"Sounds good to me," George replied. "Whatever works."

Two days later Major Barnett walked into George's office. "I don't know what you pulled," he said, " but the House finance chairman just moved ten grand into our department's budget and it's earmarked for cold case operations. You've got your trip south for the Ketchikan investigation as a start.

"The colonel says go with it and come back with some real evidence. The Ketchikan police department would love to see this case closed and somebody put in jail. It has been on their books unsolved for twenty-five years."

A broad smile crossed George Tallent's face.

"You've got a good track record on this stuff," Barnett said, "and if you think you need to talk to all three of those people then that's the way you should do it.

"I'll tell you what," Tallent said. "How about if I just go to San Diego to talk to the second husband and Chicago to talk to the suspect? I'll need to talk to the mother some more but I can do that by phone. I don't need to be looking into her eyes to know if she's telling the truth."

"OK, I'll run it by the colonel. Shouldn't be a problem with ten grand in the budget for this stuff. There'd be enough left over for a nice travel budget for more cold case investigations. I'll make sure it gets earmarked for that."

Chapter 45

THE FOLLOWING DAY MAJOR BARNETT TOLD GEORGE the trip was approved. George made the travel arrangements and called Jane Wrath's ex-husband, Cal Carpenter in Los Angeles, to set up the interview. He decided to hold off on contacting Jane Wrath until shortly after the Carpenter interview. He wanted to give her just enough notice to make her worry and build anxiety that he hoped would work in his favor. In this business, he sometimes thought, you never could predict with certainty how things might go. It was always a gamble, but he tried to make it an informed gamble.

In the third week of September, Tallent boarded a flight for the three-hour flight from Anchorage to Seattle, then caught a connecting flight for the 900-mile trip to Los Angeles. Cal Carpenter was then piloting charter flights out of Long Beach Airport and living in an apartment in Los Angeles.

George rang the doorbell and waited until the rail-thin Carpenter answered the door.

"Come in, please," the man said. "I'm glad you could make it. This thing has been bugging me ever since my wife told me how she got rid of her first husband, the guy she married before me."

George spent three hours with the man and interviewed him at length about his wife, their relationship and what she had said about her first husband. When he asked why the woman might have killed him, Carpenter replied. "I guess she just got tired of having him around, so she shot him twice, point-blank. He must have died on the spot."

"What happened after that?"

"She says she got out his ax, chopped him in pieces, put the pieces in plastic garbage bags and dropped them into the Dumpster out in the alley behind the house."

"And that was picked up when?"

"A couple of days later. The garbage truck comes up the alley, hooks up the big container and empties it into its own tank. Only takes a minute and the two-man crew usually doesn't even get out of the truck's cab. I suspect they unloaded into the incinerator at the city dump a couple of hours later. Crew probably never saw or heard anything. The guy's body parts were burned to ashes and those were never inspected."

Tallent made a mental note to ask for an excavation and examination of the ash pile. Hopefully the city's Solid Waste Services Department kept records of the dates involved in each of its ash piles. With a little luck his team might find ashes or fragments that could be examined for traces of DNA, something that would indicate that the final resting place of Scott Woburn was the Ketchikan city dump.

"Well, thank you for the information," he said as he gathered his materials from Cal Carpenter's dining room table and prepared to leave his home. "If anything else occurs to you about your wife, give me a call."

Cal raised a finger to indicate he had a question. "If you don't mind my asking, are you going to talk to Scott's mother in Los Angeles?"

"Yes, I'm going there next. Why do you ask?" George was thinking the woman's husband might be able to offer an aspect that hadn't occurred to him. It was the purpose of his next planned visit.

"She might have some of his possessions there, maybe something from when he was a kid."

"That's what I was thinking," George replied. "You never know about those things and after all these years I can't afford to miss any possibilities."

Carpenter nodded as George stood, walked through the door and closed it behind him. Cal sat grimacing, relieved that the Alaska detective might be able to get more than the slim pieces of information he was able to offer.

Margaret Woburn was in her 80s and lived in a quiet suburban area on the outskirts of Los Angeles that featured moderately expensive homes. Her husband had left California with another woman two years after their son disappeared in Alaska. The marriage had been rocky for years and the anguish from Scott's disappearance in the Far North was the final straw. She lived on a Social Security check and a small pension from her long-time employer in the telephone industry.

George rang the doorbell and was mildly surprised when an older woman strode to the door. She shouted through the glass asking who he was. George held his trooper badge and a business card to the window so the woman unlocked and opened the door. "Please come in," she said, waving him toward a seat. "And thank you for coming to Los Angeles. I am very worried about my son and, as you know, have reason to believe his wife has murdered him."

The interior of her home was nicely furnished. The woman and the detective moved to her kitchen table and talked for more than an hour. Most of what she said was either irrelevant to the case or items she had mentioned before. As the discussion came to a close, Tallent asked: "Would you have any of Scott's possessions here, anything he might have touched when he lived with you or visited here after moving away?"

The woman grimaced and thought for a moment, then brightened. "I still have a few of his toys and some of his old clothing," Mrs. Woburn said, "but they've been dusted and cleaned many times over the years. I doubt if there is anything from Scott left on them. You are welcome to take them if you want."

George followed her into a back bedroom, one that still contained a child's bunk bed and furnishings appropriate for a young boy. Several toys still sat beside the bed an on a nearby bureau. George photographed everything and made a list of the various items. He doubted that anything contained useful material but he would bring the question to the lab director in Anchorage. If the lab chief wanted to see anything he would ask Mrs. Woburn to ship it north.

As he prepared to depart, the woman said: "Oh, there are a couple of things you might be interested in. I still have his wisdom teeth from when they were extracted while he was in his late teens. They were getting painful and a dentist removed them over a couple of years. Scott offered them to me as a joke but I've kept them because they were part of my boy." She rushed back to the living room, removed a small urn-like jar from the mantle and rolled four highly-polished teeth into his hand.

George dropped two teeth into a plastic bag and handed the container with the remaining two back to the woman. "I'll just take these for the lab technicians," he said. "You can keep the other two as mementoes of your son.

"Thank you," she said, clutching the jar to her bosom.

Chapter 46

GEORGE CAUGHT A FOUR-HOUR FLIGHT from Los Angeles to Chicago, met a Chicago policewoman at the O'Hare Airport and rode with her in a cruiser to the city's Hyde Park neighborhood. Jane Wrath was then working in the alumni office at the University of Chicago and lived in an expensive apartment in the area. An attractive woman in late middle-age answered the doorbell.

"Are you Jane Wrath?" he asked.

"I am. Who are you?"

George showed his badge and said "I'm Alaska State Trooper George Tallent and this is Chicago Policewoman Margaret Tananger. We'd like to talk to you about your first husband, Scott Woburn."

The woman's face fell and she refused to look her visitors in the eye. She obviously knew what they wanted, had been expecting someone like them for many years.

"What do you want to know?" she asked, her face hanging very very low.

George glanced at Officer Tananger, the woman's face telling them a lot, then he turned back to Jane Wrath. "We have reason to believe you killed him at that cabin in Ketchikan, that you shot him, cut him up and threw the pieces into a Dumpster."

Jane Wrath shrugged, grimaced and said resignedly: "Yes, I did. It was a long time ago and I wish it hadn't happened but it did. He was a hard man to live with and the day came when I couldn't let it go on any longer. I shot him. Twice, once in the chest and once in the face. It was a terrible day and a horrible thing to do, but I couldn't help myself. I couldn't put up with him any longer. So I made it stop. Are you going to arrest me?"

"We have more investigating to do but I think it would be best if we took you into custody and keep you here in Chicago until I can get a judge to order you transferred to the Anchorage jurisdiction. I'm afraid you might be in danger of self-harm if we didn't take you to Officer Tananger's headquarters. You'll be restrained there in a holding facility until I can make arrangements to return you to Anchorage."

The woman submitted to arrest, gathered a few personal items and went with the two police officials to Officer Tananger's cruiser. At police headquarters she was led to a cell in the women's section of the lockup and George walked with Margaret Tananger to Tananger's office.

The Chicago policewoman had a surprised look on her face. "That went well," she said. "I'm surprised it was so easy."

George nodded. "The murder has been preying on the woman's conscience for years. She has mentioned it to several people, including her second husband. He reported it to us. I think she has wanted to get it out in the open for a very long time."

The two officers worked on the phone with an Anchorage judge for several hours the next day. The judge agreed with their argument and signed an order remanding Jane Wrath's custody to the Alaska State Troopers. Early the next morning the Chicago policewoman drove George and the hand-cuffed Jane Wrath to O'Hare Airport where they boarded a flight to Anchorage.

When the flight landed at Anchorage International Airport it was met by two female officers from the Anchorage Police Department. They took custody of the prisoner and escorted her to a holding facility at the Anchorage Correctional Center in Downtown Anchorage.

When he returned to his office, George handed the bag with the dead man's wisdom teeth to a lab technician. "See if you can get some DNA out of them," he told the man in the white uniform. "We don't have a body but the information could be critical if we ever find any body parts or even some usable ashes. If his remains turn up, maybe we can give the teeth back to his mother."

"There won't be much left after I run my tests," the technician warned. "I might have to grind them up to get anything useful."

"No problem," George replied. "She has two more. The important thing is to get the DNA and hang onto it for future reference."

When George received the test report on the missing man's teeth he called the trash collection service in Ketchikan and learned that the company kept careful records on where the various piles of refuse came from and when they were deposited there. One section of the dump was dedicated to trash from Jane Wrath's neighborhood. It was also able to determine approximately when and where the materials from that section of Ketchikan were deposited. That enabled the company to narrow the possibilities down to less than a quarter-acre of community garbage.

GEORGE FLEW TO KETCHIKAN AND MET WITH THE POLICE department's investigative staff. They were intrigued by the case and determined that it would be a formidable task to sort through so much trash but ashes would stand out from unburned materials and, with luck, it might be possible to find Scott Woburn's earthly remains.

The police officers and a team of volunteers were assisted by two heavy-equipment operators who sifted through the garbage for three days. They found several areas containing gray matter that appeared to be ash. Samples were taken from each and flown to the Crime Lab in Anchorage. Three days later George got a call from the lab director. "It's a match," he said, "to the ash, to the samples from the cabin and to the wisdom teeth. Same guy."

As expected, when Jane Wrath went to court the judge asked for a mental health evaluation and Mrs. Wrath was committed to a treatment facility in Seattle. Her prognosis for future recovery was considered dim.

George then returned to Anchorage and his life with Cindy. He also resumed real estate sales though his enthusiasm for that job was by then minimal. His primary focus was on the enticing possibility of a new cold case assignment from the State Troopers' Alaska Bureau of Investigation, a challenging one that would occupy both his mind and his time.

Chapter 47

———•———

WHEN HE RETURNED TO THE OFFICE NEXT DAY he approached Major Worthen's cubicle and got a warm welcoming wave.

"Do you have anything more for me?" George asked. "If not, I have one I'd like to tackle"

"What did you have in mind?" Major Worthen asked.

"The disappearance of Congressmen Rick Albert and Harley Whitney has been bugging me for years. Rick was my buddy all through school and his loss hit me pretty hard. I'd like to take a fresh look at the case, see what I can find."

"I'll need to get it cleared by the folks on high," Worthen said. "I think that might be worth doing. A lot of people have looked into it and got nowhere. But if anybody can come up with something solid, that would be you."

"Thanks Major," Tallent said. "That assignment would mean a lot to me."

Tallent started work on the project even before his approval came through for it. He worked from home after the real estate office closed and planned to write off the money he would have earned if his investigation was turned down by the people on high.

He was especially motivated to take on the case by an email he received from an old friend, a retired Alaska State Trooper then living in Phoenix. An acquaintance of the retired friend, a man who was working at the Arizona State Prison, had heard a rumor that a man serving a long sentence for armed robbery knew something that might be connected to the Alaska disappearances.

The prisoner said his former cellmate had told him a friend had asked him to smuggle a package to Alaska on an airliner three days before the two congressmen disappeared. He suspected it contained explosives. Though the report was uncorroborated, and might not even be true, it was well worth checking out.

When Tallent got word that his proposal had been approved by State Trooper leadership, he requested and received a round-trip ticket to Phoenix.

His wife Cindy laughed when he told her about the assignment. "I see," she said. "It's the middle of January in Alaska and you just happened to have to go to Phoenix for an investigation. How long have you been sitting on the case before you decided to fly to sun country to check it out. I might just ask my dad if I could go with you and buy some new display cases for his store"

A sheepish smile crossed George's face. "You could come and help me check things out," he said. "I'd be glad to pay for your plane ticket and the state would pay for our hotel room."

"Thank you for the offer," she said. "But I know how you are when you work. You would be so intense and focused on your case that you'd forget I was there."

"No I wouldn't," George countered. "I'll be doing a lot of work while I'm there but I'd also spend time with you. In fact, when I wasn't working on my case I would lavish attention on you."

"That's OK," Cindy answered. "I would like to go to Arizona with you sometime, but I would rather it wasn't when you're working on a case. I'd have to compete for your attention in a deal like that. Just keep it in mind and invite me when the time is right, maybe next year."

A relieved look crossed George's face. He was still fiercely in love with his wife but he was also intensely focused on his work, which these days involved some of the most fascinating investigations of his law enforcement career.

The next morning he left home in his personal car, parked it in the long-term parking lot at Anchorage International Airport and boarded a bus for the main terminal. There he waited anxiously until an Alaska Airlines clerk called his flight and he boarded a 737 for the long flight to Phoenix with an intermediate stop in Seattle.

The Arizona State Prison in Phoenix features a welcoming-looking exterior with red-brick columns. Its Alhambra reception area was unremarkable but Tallent was not interested in the prison; his mind was focused on Vincent Tarragon, the lifer whose former cellmate seemed to know something about the missing aircraft. The man shuffled into the reception area and took a seat on the prisoners' side of a bullet-proof panel with a large glass window and a screen through which they could talk. He was a graying man in a gray prison uniform and had deeply sad eyes.

Tallent introduced himself and asked the man: "I understand your buddy said he knows something about the airplane that disappeared in Alaska, the one with the two congressmen aboard?"

Tarragon coughed into his closed fist and responded. "Well, I can't say that for sure, but he did tell me something that might relate to it."

"OK," Tallent replied, trying to seem only modestly interested in the man's answer. "what was that?"

"He said a guy gave him a package in Los Angeles and asked him to deliver it to a man in Anchorage, a mob guy with connections to Rick Albert's wife. The one who handed it to him said to be careful because it could blow up if he shook it too much."

"And when did the mob character give him the package?"

"It was right about the time when the airplane went missing in 1972, a couple of days before that."

"Did he know anything about the explosive in the package?" George asked.

"He said he thought it was C-4 or something like that."

"Did he mention C-4 specifically?"

"Yeah, I remember that. It stuck in my mind. I don't know anything about explosives but I do know that C-4 is bad shit."

George scribbled furiously in his notebook. "What was his name and where is he now?"

Tarragon grimaced. "His name *was* Al Pocaccio but he's dead now, got shot a couple of days after he got out of here and went back to California."

"What do you know about the shooting?"

"Not much," the prisoner replied. "It was on the news at the time because he got shot in the bleachers at a major league baseball game. They talked about it on TV. Made me wonder if I really want to get released. It's dangerous out there these days."

Tallent smiled at the remark. Vincent Tarragon was in prison for the horrendous rape and murder of a teenage girl in New Mexico. There was little chance he would ever be released.

"Anything else you can tell me about him?"

"Not that I can think of. He didn't talk about himself much. I don't think anybody here got any information out of him. Even when he was all-out jabbering he would clam up if anybody asked him a question. He was high on something when he told me about smuggling that package."

Tallent tried a few more questions but the answers were all similar. Later that day he called California State Police headquarters in Sacramento and talked to a sergeant in its records department.

The sergeant called up a file on his computer screen and said: "Pocaccio was a small-time hood who was always broke. He got killed a few days after he got back here from Phoenix. We never learned who knocked him off or why, though we think it might have been someone sent to LA by the Seattle mob. It was obviously somebody who was waiting for him to get back into town. And Albert's ex-wife took up with a mob guy in Anchorage after she divorced Rick. She married him just a few months after Rick's disappearance."

George scribbled a few notes, then asked: "Anything else you can tell me about him?"

"Well, yeah. Pocaccio had a long rap sheet and you are welcome to it. We don't like to have computer files going around the internet but if you send me a mailing address I'll print it out and send you a hard copy."

"Thanks," Tallent said. "I'd like to know more about him though the information may not be what I'm looking for. Pocaccio was apparently a courier for somebody who might or might not have been involved in the case I'm working on. It's worth going through his file to see if any connections stand out. That smuggled bomb makes my hair stand on end."

Chapter 48

Tallent gave the California sergeant his office address in Anchorage and hung up. That night at dinner he took a pensive sip of wine and said to Cindy: "You know, I'm convinced that the plane with Rick Albert and the others went down on Columbia Glacier. I have no evidence to that effect but when I flew over the glacier after they disappeared I had this very strong feeling that he was down there somewhere."

"Is there any way to check it out?" she asked. "Can you get in there on the surface?"

"It wouldn't be easy," he replied. "The glacier has changed a lot since the plane disappeared in 1972."

"Changed how?" Cindy asked.

"The terminus has retreated about ten miles and the glacier's surface is about 1,600 feet lower than it was then. It's a much different place now than it was at that time."

"Are you going to go take a look at it?" she asked.

"I have to," he replied. "I'm thinking I'll go in with a small party, probably in a helicopter."

"Can I come?" she asked. Cindy was an athletic woman and an occasional mountain climber.

"No way," George replied. "I'd be worried about you the whole time and that would be a distraction from my job."

"Well then, you be careful."

"I will indeed."

Two weeks later Tallent and two other state troopers, both experienced climbers, flew to Columbia Glacier in a department helicopter piloted by an Alaska State Trooper. They landed on a flat rock outcrop at the edge of the ice and midway up the glacier's length. Wearing crampons and climbing gear the three men made their way across the glacial surface, working from one edge to the other and studying the ice as they went.

After an hour, one waved to Tallent and pointed to the ice at his feet. Tallent made his way to the man's side and peered into the shallow crevasse. Several feet down and visible through a patch of clear ice was something darker than the surrounding ice.

"What is it?" George asked.

"Can't tell," his companion said. "But it looks like something solid."

George sat on the ice surface with his feet dangling in the crevasse. He began chipping at a wall below with his ice ax. The buried object was only about three inches from the edge of the ice and he soon was able to remove it from the crevasse.

"It's a piece of metal," he said. "Hopefully the lab can tell us what it's from."

Later that day George drove to the Crime Lab and left the metal object with a technician. That night he told Cindy he had a strong suspicion that the metal was from the plane that had carried Rick Albert and Harley Whitney the day they disappeared. Two days later the technician called to say that the metal appeared to be part of the tail structure of a light aircraft.

"And one very important item," the technician said. "A test just came back indicating there is a trace amount of explosive residue embedded in the metal. It has been sitting in that ice for a lot of years and there isn't much left of it, but it's definitely the real thing."

"Was it C4?" George asked.

"It was indeed," the technician said.

GEORGE IMMEDIATELY BEGAN ORGANIZING a larger search party to return to the surface of Columbia Glacier and resume the search. That time they recovered several small items, two more pieces of the aircraft and one tiny item that the lab confirmed to be a broken piece of a congressional pin.

George called Rick's widow. "We found it," he said. "The search turned up a small part of the plane."

"Oh-my-god," she said, stretching the words. "I can't believe after all this time."

"There's more," he said. "We found part of the pin that Rick customarily wore wherever he went. The congressional membership pin. It could have been part of Harley Whitney's pin but Whitney didn't wear his pin all the time the way Rick did. Whitney was more likely to wear his when he was in Washington."

George said the pin fragment would have to remain in state custody until the investigation was formally closed. At that time they could release it to her. He told her it would probably take at least several months, perhaps more. He thought to himself that the case would close eventually but only after he found out who placed the bomb on the aircraft and why—and made sure the perpetrators were brought to justice in an Alaska court.

Chapter 49

———•———

ONE AFTERNOON GEORGE DROVE TO AST headquarters, entered and rapped on Walt Gilmour's office door.

"Hello, there, George," Gilmour said, "to what do I owe the pleasure?"

"Afternoon, Major," George replied. "I just wanted to noodle a bit about Rick Albert."

"Anything special?"

"Well, for one thing I'm trying to get straight in my mind why Rick was flying over Columbia Glacier."

"Could have been any number or reasons, obviously, one being the fact that Harley Whitney's son went to Columbia University. He might have asked Rick to swing over the glacier just so he could take a peek—and tell his son he did."

George scratched his chin as his mind worked with the thought. "That's new information to me," he said. "It's not in the family section of the official folder."

"The boy died in his 20s," Gilmour said. "when Whitney was only about 45. The kid was a real up-and-comer but was killed in a car crash. Whitney took it pretty hard. I think the boy was his only family by the time he died."

"It's a good thing they did divert over the glacier," George said. "If that bomb had gone off when they were over the Gulf of Alaska the wreckage would be a mile under the water surface. We would never have found anything."

"Why would anyone put a bomb on that airplane?" Gilmour asked. "And was it intended to kill Rick Tallent or Harley Whitney?"

"Or both," George added.

"That seems a stretch," Gilmour said, "but check it out. Check out all the possibilities. It's your investigation and the trail has long gone cold but go wherever it takes you and let me know if you need anything.

"Will do," George said as he turned and headed back out the door, his mind churning.

Two nights later George returned home deep in thought. Cindy could see his obvious distraction as soon as he entered the kitchen where she was preparing their dinner.

"Now what?" she asked.

George was about to give his usual admonition when Cindy ran a finger across her lips indicating they were sealed.

"Joe Hamel from the FBI office here did a little digging in the congressional records and came across some interesting stuff. Apparently in the month before their plane crashed Rick's wife Myrlie and Harley Whitney's wife Alice spent a lot of time on the phone together."

"Any idea what they were talking about?" Cindy asked.

"No, but there is something about the deal that you won't believe," George replied.

"Uh huh," she said, her voice inquisitive.

"This has never come out before," George said, "but at the time the plane crashed the FBI was tapping Rick's home phone. They were convinced he was into some sleazy business in New Delhi and got a judge to authorize the wiretap."

"What kind of sleazy business?"

"My buddy wouldn't tell me that," George replied. "He just wanted me to know that the records of the conversations are in Washington. The FBI at the time was only interested in Rick's conversations with his contact in New Delhi but they taped every-thing including Myrlie's home phone calls while Rick was at work. And some of those were apparently very interesting."

"Now what?" Cindy asked. "Can they send you transcripts or copies of the tape?"

"No, neither one," George said, "not without a court order."

"Can you get a court order?"

"I don't have enough solid information for that. I'll have to go to Washington. The FBI will let me read the transcripts and take notes, but that's all at this point."

"Need any help getting packed or making arrangements?" Cindy offered.

"Thanks but I can use the distraction of doing that stuff myself," George replied. "That plane crash has been on my mind for more than twenty years. And it has really been bugging me lately since this stuff came up."

IN WASHINGTON GEORGE SAT WITH THE FBI briefer almost liter-ally with his mouth hanging open.

"The strangest part of the whole package," the briefer said, "is that Myrlie Albert and Alice Whitney had put together a deal with their mob contact to kill their husbands."

"You are shitting me," George muttered.

"I shit you not," the briefer replied. "Evidently they were count-ing on the likelihood that the truth would never come out. Alice had been sleeping with the mob guy and later married him. Both were furious with their husbands because the guys were screwing every bimbo they could find in Washington, and there are quite a few, believe it or not. Evidently some of those congressional offices were way sleazier than even the more cynical members of the pub-lic could imagine. Sometime before the bomb was planted the two wives managed to draw money out of their bank accounts and send it to their contact in the Middle East. Naturally they got it all back when the insurance checks came.

"Harley Whitney was in Alaska because he knew that his wife was on the phone constantly with Myrlie Albert. He was convinced that the two women were cooking something up and was hoping he and Rick could figure it out if they could noodle the issue while away from the distractions of Washington."

"And it all came apart on them"

"It did indeed."

TOM BRENNAN HAS LIVED IN ALASKA for more than a half-century working as a newspaper reporter, editor and columnist—and writing seven books. He has had a front-row seat for much of what has happened in the state throughout that time. That unique perspective has had an important and valuable impact on his writing, an impact that is reflected in his work. Born in Massachusetts, Tom moved to Alaska with his wife Marnie in 1967 in search of adventure. The couple arrived just as oil was being discovered on Alaska's North Slope, a historic find that has provided the base for Alaska's economy and a draw for pioneering young people in the years since.